The Guardians

Book 1: The Watchers in the Rock

Shaldon is a real village and the regatta an annual event held there in August. Many of the businesses mentioned in the book are also real. The genuine Duckman of Shaldon regatta will gladly sell you a number for the annual duck race and is nothing like the impostor in this book. However, all other events and characters are fictitious and any resemblance to any persons living or dead completely coincidental.

British Library Cataloguing-In-Publication Data
A Record of This Publication is available
from the British Library

ISBN 978-184685-1483

First Published 2007 by
Cadenza Press in association with Exposure Publishing
an imprint of Diggory Press: Ltd
Three Rivers, Minions, Liskeard, Cornwall PL14 5LE

For details of other books published by Cadenza Press
please go to www.cadenzapress.co.uk
or email info@cadenzapress.co.uk

To my wife who always believed in this story

Chapter One

'Don't look behind you. I said don't look.' James was sitting on the beach and heard the crunch of sand and shingle as someone sat a few yards behind him.

It was a boy's voice, James thought. The temptation to look almost overcame him, but was stilled by another urgent whisper:

'Don't turn around, just listen. Look straight ahead.'

James stared in front of him. He was facing Teignmouth docks. A large ship tooted. It was high tide and the vessel would probably be on its way soon, carrying its cargo of clay.

'Don't look, and try to pretend we're not talking, or else they'll see and hear us.'

'Who?' James gazed steadily at the sand when he spoke, so no one could see the word being spoken.

'The mechanicals. Those two seagulls. Pick up a stone. Not a boulder, stupid, if you throw that they'll think you're attacking them, and they'll peck your eyes out.'

James released the rock he had scooped up and selected a small red pebble, part of the sandstone from the cliffs that framed Shaldon.

'Now just turn casually to your left and throw it very gently in the general direction of the two seagulls that you'll see there.'

James did as he was told. Two grey seagulls with brown speckled heads flapped into the air and landed again.

'Mechanicals?'

'There's six of them. Sent by the Watchers in the rock. Those two patrolling over there are Digger and Drum.'

James felt nervous, the boy was obviously mad. The beach was busy that morning in the run up to Shaldon regatta. His parents were sitting on the sand perhaps thirty yards away, waiting for the ferry to take them all to Teignmouth, where the plan was to get some cakes from Luder's Patisserie and ice cream from the Pier. His dog Einstein was with them, sitting and staring at the seagulls. He felt reassured by their presence and the numbers of people immediately around. Surely nothing could happen in such a public place? All he needed to do was walk casually over towards his parents and…

'I have to move,' continued the boy, 'or the mechanicals will get suspicious and realise I am communicating with you. They are never more than twenty paces away from me, watching, listening, and reporting to the Watchers. They'll get me soon. They know me so well. They should, of course. They never let anyone escape. You've got to meet me tonight at sunset. Here. It is most important.'

'Yeah, sure,' said James, 'I'll be here.'

'Don't humour me.' The boy spoke sharply. 'I'm not mad. If I can prove to you the seagulls are watching me… following me… will you meet me this evening? I can't stand this any longer. I wish I'd never escaped.'

'The Watchers, where are they?' James kept his voice low and calm.

'In the rock, of course. I said before. Stop talking, Digger and Drum are staring at you. Now watch.'

All of a sudden there was a crunch of shingle and the soft squidge of sand as the person behind stood up. Then James caught a glimpse of a boy about the same age as him, fairly short and dressed in a shapeless red top and blue trousers, who sprinted past, scattering the passengers from the ferry who were just disembarking.

A horn sounded: the clay ship was directly in front, bows pointing at the beach before it executed its sharp turn towards the sea, the pilot boat bobbing in attendance.

The figure was now in the water and swimming strongly. The seagulls lifted into the air and hovered over the boy, who changed direction. The seagulls followed. James stood up. The sun burnt his neck.

Then the boy changed direction again, in a long exaggerated curve. The seagulls followed and dived at the figure, screeching furiously. Once again the boy changed direction, heading for a dinghy that was moored securely to a red buoy. He reached the side of it and in one smooth movement clambered aboard. He picked up the oars that must have been lying in the bottom, and slipped them over the rowlocks. As he did so the seagulls attacked, dropping on his head, clutching his hair, screeching wildly and incessantly, as if they were demented.

'What on earth is happening?' Mum was staring at the scene unfolding in front as James joined her. 'That poor boy!' James ran along the beach, picked up a stone and threw it at the figures, but it fell far short. The boy was desperately trying to undo the painter, but the birds were now attacking his hands. Another two seagulls, grey with brown speckled heads arrived, cawing angrily, and joined the attack.

'Six of them, he said,' muttered James. 'That's four.' Einstein was barking furiously, straining at the lead, eager to get at the seagulls.

The boy dived into the water from the dinghy and started swimming back to shore. The attack ceased abruptly, but the birds wheeled overhead screeching. The boy had regained the beach and sat at the waters edge, shivering and shaking. A man and woman came over to speak to him but were waved away.

'Six, he said' James muttered again, 'that's four.' He walked up the gangplank to the ferry, joining his parents, and sat on the varnished seat facing towards the estuary mouth, where he could still keep the figure in view. Two of the seagulls were circling overhead. Two more were pacing around the boy, looking for all the world as if they were jailers. One of them dug furiously in the sand, scratching and tearing at a mussel, the other stood on one leg, drumming its other against a rock.

'There's four,' murmured James to himself again. 'Four proves nothing.' He felt relieved, his half promise now looking foolish. The boy's insistence fading in the reality of a hot crowded summers afternoon. He glanced up towards the person strolling round the boat collecting fares. Behind him, standing on the ship's side staring hard at him, were the remaining two seagulls. They threw back their heads and a screeching cry bubbled in their throats.

'And that's six,' said James, swallowing nervously. 'Just like he said.'

Chapter Two

IT HAD been a blistering day again, one of many in a Mediterranean-like summer. It was close to sunset, but the beach was still alive with people sitting on the sand, strolling, or paddling on the edge of the river. Most of the boats were lying tipped on their sides, as the tide had receded. The Salty was fully exposed, looking more like a great brown field than an island that disappeared under the waves every few hours. Its huge beds of mussels lay encased in a blanket of seagulls, like a dirty white duvet. The seagulls hopped up and down and flew into the air and landed again, as they searched for a tasty morsel. But now the tide was on the turn.

At this stage it was running strongly as it pushed into the narrow gap between the Point at Teignmouth and the Ness, the red sandstone cliffs at the seaward end of the river beach at Shaldon. Two of the finest vantage points in all of Devon. The Ness, for its panoramic elevated views of Lyme bay, and the Point for its flatter perspective from sea level, which gave unrivalled views of the big ships as they turned and twisted up the winding channel into Teignmouth docks.

'I'm going for a row,' James said to his parents that evening. 'I'm meeting Mugsy.' The next day was the official start of the ten day long Shaldon regatta. The opening event was the long distance row from Dawlish to Shaldon. James had entered with Mugsy, his best friend, in the under 16's.

'Don't forget your life jacket.'

'Oh, mum...'' James hated wearing his life jacket, feeling it restricted his rowing.

'If you don't wear it you can't go, you know mum's rules, which in this case happen to be the same as the regatta rules, it will be good practice. You know you won't be allowed in the race unless you're wearing one, they're very particular about safety.' She had picked up the well thumbed regatta race programme and read, "all persons of 14 years and under to wear a life jacket."

'Ok, I'll go and get it, I'll be out for an hour or so.'

'It'll be dark by then,' said dad, looking up from his newspaper, 'you'll need to rig up some searchlights.'

James had walked thoughtfully down the steps to the garage and entered his workshop, where he took the lifejacket from its hook and slipped it on. It was getting tight; he would need the next size up soon. He smiled to himself; it should be easy to get mum to pay for that on the grounds of safety, rather than have to find it from his own pocket money.

He was halfway down the garden when dad shouted from the balcony;

'Haven't you forgotten something rather essential for rowing?'

James looked at him blankly, his thoughts already down on the beach wondering if the boy would turn up.

'Or are you going to use your hands? It won't go very fast.'

'Eh?' said James vaguely.

'Your oars, you can't row without oars. At least not in my day you couldn't'

'Oh, yes,' James retraced his steps and collected the oars, smooth, well-varnished and glistening in the late sun. He balanced one in each hand and headed for the garden gate again.

'Have a good row.'

'Thanks,' James called back over his shoulder.

He walked down the hill and through the Botanical gardens, where he could see the vast expanse of the Salty, and just beyond it the blue warehouses of the docks. One ship was still moored, a large black vessel with red superstructure. A gantry ran down its spine that contained cranes and a winch. It was low in the water. It must be full of the local clay that was shipped all over the world. The next high tide and it would probably be off.

He had arranged to meet Mugsy in the ferry shelter just in front of the Beachcomber café. He hadn't told him of his strange encounter on the beach, but had phoned to suggest they needed a last practice row.

There were a lot of people just walking aimlessly in the road. There was no sign of the stranger. The garden of the Beachcomber, which overlooked the beach, was packed with people eating and drinking. James walked across the road and on to the sand, glancing inside the ferry shelter. Mugsy wasn't there yet, James was a little early and Mugsy was not the most punctual of people. He always used to be late for school and had carried the habit into his social life.

James turned towards where his boat was dragged up to the top of the beach, just in front of the Ferryboat Inns' beer garden. That was also packed, people sitting tight against each other on the wooden benches talking loudly. A harassed-looking waitress was bearing out great platefuls of food, skilfully evading the knots of

9

people standing in her way. The regatta was very popular and a much loved institution amongst the people who participated year after year, and with those who just came to watch what were, in effect, an adult version of school sports day.

There was a new Duck Man this year. His job was to roam the beach and streets of Shaldon to sell numbers that related to those on the bottom of a yellow plastic duck. These were released on the last Sunday of the regatta from large nets tipped from a rowing boat at the mouth of the estuary. The tide swept the ducks in like a great wave of yellow custard towards the finishing line, or so the theory went, as a lot ended up on either shore. He enjoyed the recovery expedition when children rowed out to collect the ducks that had passed the finishing line, using their hands to scoop their treasure into the safety of their boats. Their prize was 5 pence per duck recovered.

He kept his hands in his pocket as the Duck Man approached. The old one, who had been doing the job for as long as James could remember, had been replaced this year by someone different. The old one had a horn slung round his neck, which he tooted to gain attention. James liked him; he had a twinkle in his eye and a knack of extracting money from the pockets of the most recalcitrant holidaymaker or resident.

James fingered the £1 coin in his pocket. This was for the grand draw tickets, not the duck race. He already had two regatta tickets but badly wanted to win first prize, a brand new Regatta dinghy, together with oars. It would cost over £700 to buy new, and there was no way he could ever save that much money. His current dinghy, which had been bought with birthday, pocket and Christmas money, together with cash from various odd jobs his parents had invented, was nice enough, but showed its age. Earlier in the summer Dad had helped to replace the rotten cross bar, needed so he could brace his feet against it in order to gain more purchase as he rowed.

'Ducks, get your lovely ducks here, choose your numbers,' a couple of visitors proffered money, but the Duck man was looking beyond them, his eyes sweeping the beach as if looking for something.

'There you are, professor,' Mugsy came up from behind and slapped James playfully on the back. 'Have you seen Geraldine? I asked her to come along and time us.'

'Oh, they've arrived, have they? No, I haven't seen her since last year. Listen, I've got...' he broke off. 'There he is!'

'Who?'

'The boy. The one in the red top and blue trousers.'

Mugsy looked over. 'Oh him, the drizzoid.'

'The what?'

'Drizzoid - that's what we call dreamers at our school.'

James mentally filed the term away to introduce at the grammar school to which he had gone last year; Mugsy, who was brilliant at sports but less interested in academic subjects, had opted for the big school in Teignmouth.

'A school's a school.' he had said, 'why have the drag of getting on a coach when I can just walk from my home to my school? It's really cool there.'

It was strange not to sit next to him in class, which they had done since their first day at Shaldon primary when they were both rising 5's.

'You know him, then?' quizzed James. 'The boy?'

'I heard Alex and his gang talking to him. He approached them yesterday when they were jumping into the river down at the quay, showing off to the visitors. A mega drizzoid they called him, completely away with the fairies. Then when Alex didn't want to know he came over to me and tried to spin some silly yarn. Has he been speaking to you? You didn't believe him and his tales of robot seagulls, Romans and mysterious watchers? Alex said they nearly threw him in the water, but he was jolly strong and managed to pull away from them. That's it! I remember now, he told them they didn't have much longer unless they listened to him, then he told me the same. Didn't you think he was talking complete nonsense then?'

James looked thoughtful. 'Yes. No. I don't know, he seemed believable and said that if he showed he was being followed would I meet him this evening. I've got to keep my promise. Will you come with me? I'm going to walk towards the Ness a bit, it'll be a lot quieter over there. Whatever you do, don't speak to the boy or acknowledge him in any way, or the birds might attack us as well as him.' Mugsy raised his eyebrows but said nothing.

The two walked off casually towards the far end of the river beach, threading their way through the visitors. A voice called out;

'You coming for a row, professor?' There was a slight drawn out intonation to the last word - gently mocking. 'You're going to need all the practice you can get if you're going to beat me. A boat not rotting where she's lying would help too! You can't expect to do anything with that heap, other than hope you can swim well.'

James suppressed his anger and spoke calmly. 'A bit later perhaps, Alex,' he walked past the boy, who was sitting by his own brand new regatta dinghy with two of his friends.

'Hi, Bas, hello, Ritchie, you all right?' said James politely as they walked past the group and along the beach towards the boy, who had sat down well away from the crowds.

With Mugsy trailing behind, he walked well in front of the boy and crouched on the sand, not acknowledging the presence of the other. The two seagulls looked up, hopped on their legs, gave a screech then resumed their activities, one digging in the sand, the other drumming its foot against a rock.

James stood up again, walked to the sea, picked up a pebble, weighed it carefully in his hand and threw it into the water. Then he picked up another and skimmed it into the quickening tide. The main beach was perfectly safe, but it was unwise to bathe at this state of the tide so close to the estuary mouth. At this stage the water came sweeping in, but it was ideal for rowers, providing real exercise as they pulled hard to escape its effects and gain the open sea from the safety of the harbour. As he skimmed the pebble James glanced up the beach towards the village.

The Duck Man was walking quickly towards them, making no effort to sell his duck numbers. Another figure, which James thought looked vaguely like the strange boy, was a few yards behind him.

'Why are you here, Duck Man?' murmured James to himself, 'You don't seem very interested in doing your job.'

James sat back down with Mugsy, who had occupied himself by digging a hole in the sand with his hands. A voice came softly from behind them.

'I've got the key... you must keep it safe. Let no one else have it. Atlantis. The great cities of Mesopotamia, The Roman Empire. All gone... all destroyed. Now it's your civilisation's turn. The Guardians. I overheard the Watchers say that they'll return soon. They need the key to get in.'

'Drizzoid,' murmured Mugsy gently to James. 'Mega drizzoid, what did I tell you? Let's get out of here.'

The boy continued. 'I can't keep running. I've nowhere to go, and wherever I go the mechanicals follow. It's only a matter of time before the Watchers get me back. I wanted to warn your civilisation, but no one seems to want to listen, they all think I'm mad.'

Mugsy shifted uncomfortably but didn't say anything.

'Where can I leave it? The key? I can't give it to you openly, the mechanicals are watching and you will become their target. Somewhere close though, I don't have much time left, somewhere...' the voice tailed off, 'it's him, it's one of the Watchers.'

James turned slowly, there was one man sitting down on the beach throwing stones, but where was the Duck Man? There! Coming round behind the boy... he was very close.

James spoke softly. 'The Lucy Ann - my boat - leave it under there; it's on the beach just in front of the Ferry Boat Inn.'

A crowd of holidaymakers rattled down the steps on to the beach clutching cricket gear. The boy stood up and joined them, walking briskly, the Duck Man marooned on the wrong side of the crowd.

The two seagulls lifted into the air screaming. The Duck Man stopped, turned and followed the group down the beach, keeping pace with the boy opposite.

Two more seagulls swooped down. James raised an oar defensively but they flew over his head and joined Digger and Drum, hovering over the boy, screaming and screeching and marking out his position clearly amongst the melee.

The cricketers stopped short of the Lucy Ann, and one man started to set up some stumps in the sand, another bounced a tennis ball on his bat. The boy joined a smaller knot of people who had just arrived from the ferry and were making for the beach entrance to the Ferry Boat Inn. The boy disappeared for a few moments, then reappeared, running strongly straight towards the sea, he reached the edge and plunged in to the water. He swam strongly towards the entrance to the estuary but the tide - now at full gallop - forced him back, sweeping him along the course of the river as it curved round by Teignmouth back beach. He disappeared under the surface and just for a second James imagined he saw something else in the water, something white that brushed against him. 'Shark!' he cried involuntarily, then felt foolish and was glad no one had heard.

Mugsy certainly hadn't heard him, he was racing towards the water, kicking off his shoes as he went. James was just behind, caught his arm and held it firmly.

'No, Mugsy, don't go in, you'll be swept away!' Mugsy hesitated, and as he did so several rowing boats converged on the spot where the boy had disappeared under the water. They paddled around for a few minutes, men yelling, a woman leaning dangerously over the side of one, peering intently into the depths. Someone took their life jacket off and threw it into the water in the forlorn hope that an arm might emerge from the swirling current and grab it. Another man stuck in an oar and twirled it violently around, as if hoping to hook out a figure. Then the inshore lifeboat arrived, called by someone on the beach with a mobile phone.

James collapsed onto the sand, brushed away a tear with the back of his hand and bit his lip, shaking violently with the shock. He glanced up the beach. The Duck Man had gone. He looked beyond the lifeboat and stared out to sea. There were six seagulls, grey with brown speckled heads, flying together inches above the sea towards the Ness, they screeched noisily as they followed the channel. They let an up draught catch their wings to take them to the top of the cliff where they disappeared from view.

Chapter Three

THE apparent drowning cast a pall over the start of the regatta, but the next day the beach gradually filled, the teashops became busy and the shops crowded, with many more people arriving on the ferry from Teignmouth than departing on it. The sun shone strongly and numerous boats swept in and out of the estuary, some going out to sea for the day fishing for sea bass and mackerel. A bigger boat with a blue dolphin emblazoned on its side thudded its way out, crowded with visitors hoping to catch a glimpse of the dolphins. Some small yachts pottered into Lyme Bay using their outboards, and powerful speedboats, together with some jet bikes, motored out ready to visit some of the coves between Shaldon and Babbacombe, accessible only by sea.

A few larger yachts motored out, hoping to catch a breath of breeze in order to fill their sails, which hung limp as the blue flags on Shaldon beach, which bore the legend "Shaldon Regatta", each erected on one of four moveable steel flag posts. The structures stood close to two rectangular blue tents, open at one side, where officials and those selling programmes and tickets and accepting entry forms for the various races, were located. Several Union Jacks hung equally limply at the back of the river beach, mixed in with the coloured bunting that lined the Strand then wove its way towards the Village Green.

The rowing race from Dawlish back to Shaldon was at 5.30pm, some one and a half hours after low tide, so the rowers would be assisted by the quickening current as they entered the estuary mouth.

'Are you having a practice row this morning?' asked Mum at breakfast.

'Yes, I'm meeting Mugsy and Geraldine around 10, she phoned this morning. We want to row before it gets too hot.'

'Are you OK?' asked Mum gently, ' you seem quiet this morning.'

'No, I'm fine.'

'You didn't know that boy who drowned did you? He didn't go to school with you or play in your cricket team or anything?'

'No,' said James, 'not know him as such, that is, I'd spoken to him when we were in the ferry queue, and again last night on the beach, just before he... just before he ran into the water. But I've no idea who he was, a visitor I assume. He certainly wasn't from round here, one of us would have recognised him.'

'Yes, I suppose it must have been a visitor. It sounded like the same boy that was mobbed by those dreadful seagulls when we were waiting to get on the ferry. Was it?'

'Yes,' agreed James.

'I went down to the beach first thing this morning and threw in a flower for him on to the waves.'

James nodded and bit his lip, 'that's nice.'

'I also said a poem, he was so young and no one seems to have come forward to say they knew him, so I thought someone needed to show they cared.'

James felt a tear forming and turned away so his mother wouldn't see it.

'Would you like to hear it?' James got his love of poetry from his parents, although he rarely talked about it to his friends, it wasn't as cool as being in the school football team, or knowing how to avoid going on the weekly cross country run.

'Yes, I'd like to. Go ahead.'

Mum went to her handbag and got out a piece of paper. 'I don't know who it's by, but it gives me comfort at difficult times.' She cleared her throat and spoke softly;

"Do not stand at my grave and weep
I am not there I do not sleep
I am a thousand winds that blow
I am the diamond glints on snow
I am the sunlight on ripened grain
I am the gentle autumn rain.

When you awaken in the mornings hush
I am the swift uplifting rush
Of quiet birds in circled flight
I am the soft stars that shine at night
Do not stand at my grave and cry
I am not there I did not die."

There was a silence then James said, 'Mum... about those seagulls.'

Just then, as if on cue, Einstein ran through the house barking furiously and hurled herself in rage at the balcony, scrabbling at the patio door, which wasn't open far enough for her to get out.

'Still, we don't need to worry too much about seagulls with Einstein around,' said mum laughing, the sombre mood broken. 'She really seems to hate them with a passion, doesn't she? She nearly caught those two just then.'

'Two,' said James, 'two seagulls, where? Are you sure?'

'Yes, they were sitting on the balcony rail.'

'Were they grey with… with…'

'Are you sure you're OK, dear? You've gone pale. Perhaps it's delayed shock, or too much sun, it's been more like the French Riviera than the English Riviera for large parts of this summer. It was those two gulls over there, sitting on the garage roof trying to get away from Einstein.'

James looked over, 'they're plain white ones, it's OK, it's not… that is, I must be getting off or we'll be rowing in heat that makes the Sahara seem like the North Pole.'

Mum smiled, 'What time will you be back?'

'By lunch, we'll row for an hour or so, we don't want to be too good or it won't be fair on the others.'

When James got down to the beach he found Mugsy standing by the Lucy Ann, eating an ice cream. A tall girl with red hair and freckles was standing next to him.

'Geraldine?'

'Didn't you recognise me? It's only been a year.' She gave him a little kiss on the cheek. James wiped it away

'When did you arrive?'

'Yesterday afternoon. We're here for two weeks as usual. You know my parents never miss the regatta. They've entered for practically everything this year. Wasn't it terrible that boy drowning like that? Have they found his…'

'His body?' finished James, 'no, not yet, the tide would have taken it up past Coombe cellars to Newton Abbott, I guess.'

Geraldine shivered. 'Sorry I didn't come to meet you yesterday evening, mum wanted me to unpack, then we had dinner. Still, I'm here now. Where's the roller?'

Mugsy walked a few paces along the sand and burrowed under another boat.

'It's here behind this dinghy, I noticed it earlier.' He tugged it out and pulled it across the sand, placed it in front of the Lucy Ann's bow, then walked slowly backwards, unfurling the device, a series of plastic cylinders fastened within a wire frame.

'Not too far to push the old tub today,' said Geraldine brightly, 'the tide seems quite high, it's well up the beach. I hate really low tides, you almost have to push the boat to Teignmouth to find any water.'

James laughed; it was good to see Geraldine again.

'Didn't you recognise me just now?'

'Of course I did,' said James blushing again, 'you just looked taller, and you've… you've filled out since last year.'

'You mean I'm fat,' said Geraldine mockingly, looking at him mouth half open, eyes twinkling. Then she rolled her eyes in the way they had all practiced last summer, and they both laughed.

Mugsy strode back up the beach. 'What's the joke?'

'Nothing, come on, grab that side of the boat, I'll go this side. Gerry, will you push at the stern?'

The boat rattled over the rollers and dropped into the sea with a satisfying splash, where it bobbed gently in the light swell.

'Who said you could use the ramp?' an angry voice shouted at them.

James looked up, 'it's for anyone to use Alex, you know that. What's the problem?'

'The problem is we were just about to use it ourselves when Mugsy stole it.'

'I did not,' said Mugsy indignantly, 'how did I know you were going to use it, you weren't anywhere near? I'm not a mind reader, you know.'

'I'm sorry, Alex,' called Geraldine sweetly, 'it was my fault, I was eager to get the Lucy Ann launched, it's been a year since I saw her in the water.'

'Oh, it's you.' Alex walked down the beach and when he spoke again his tone had changed completely. 'That's OK. How are you? It's good to see you again.'

'Fine, thank you. It's nice to see you again. Is that the new boat I've heard about? She's a beauty, you must be very proud of her.'

Mugsy looked at James and made a face, James smiled back. Alex had always had a soft spot for Geraldine.

'Yes, my dad got her for me last month. She's nice, it's a shame the race has to be spoilt by allowing old wrecks in, it brings down the whole tone of the regatta.' He looked pointedly at the Lucy Ann.

'Well, I'm sure you'll row to the best of your ability,' said Geraldine, 'see you later.'

'He was drooling,' said Mugsy grinning broadly as Alex trudged up the beach pulling the roller behind him.

'Never mind that,' said Geraldine, 'are you two going to have a practice row? You'll have to work really hard if you want to beat him and Bas.'

***

Shaldon lies at the seaward end of the river Teign which starts its life high on Dartmoor which provides a distant backdrop to the village. A picturesque cluster of mainly Victorian and Georgian houses lines a main street interspersed with all the necessities of life, from Churches to Tea rooms with a village green watched over by a war memorial.

A small zoo nestles into the Cliffs adjacent to a smugglers tunnel, which cuts through the heart of the Ness to another beach, this one facing the sea.

James swivelled round from his vantage point in the Botanical Gardens. A seagull screeched. James scanned the sky, then located it sitting on a large fuchsia bush, swaying precariously on the thin branches. Ever since the tragic accident he had looked closely at every seagull strutting on the beach or circling in the air. It was grey. He looked round quickly to locate its partner, but there was no sign of it. He turned back and stared hard at the gull, which pecked at a seedpod and dropped it. It sprang to the floor and hopped on one leg to retrieve it. James held his breath then let it out in a great sigh. Its head was grey as well, not brown and speckled. He looked at his watch; he had been daydreaming for too long, it was time to make a move. He gazed beyond

23

Teignmouth to the sea, picking out the route for the first race.

Teignmouth has a gently sloping beach of red sand backed by an elegant promenade and gracious terraces. The pier and theatre take centre stage on the promenade, before it sweeps away to Dawlish, lined by a sea wall which protects Brunel's great scenic railway.

James strode down the hill whistling tunelessly, clutching his set of oars and wearing his life jacket. At the bottom he went straight across the road and onto the sand next to the ferry shelter. Normally dinghies were pulled up here, but they had been moved in readiness for the beach games.

It was crowded with visitors and locals. Many people were clutching oars. Rowing was hugely popular in Teignmouth and Shaldon, with numerous rowing clubs sponsored by local companies and pubs. The traditional Sunday start to the regatta always began with the long distance row from Dawlish breakwater to Shaldon.

'Mugsy! Mugsy,' James shouted and waved his oars. Mugsy looked up and waved back as James threaded his way through the crowds.

'Is Gerry here yet?' he asked.

Mugsy inclined his head, 'She's chatting to one of the captains of the spectator boats.'

'Oh, good, she'd get a better view of the whole race from a boat rather than standing on the beach. You got in our entry form OK?'

Mugsy clasped his hand to his mouth 'Oh no! I knew there was something I was supposed to do.' He saw the look on James's face and said hastily, 'it's OK,

I'm just joking, I was standing right behind Alex in the queue. He was boasting to all and sundry that he was bound to win.'

'He always does,' said James gloomily, 'well he has for the last two years running.'

'He's a jolly good rower,' conceded Mugsy reluctantly, 'and Bas has always been a power house on the other oar.'

'Yes,' agreed James grudgingly, 'but you've put on a lot of weight in the last year or so - pure muscle of course,' he continued hastily, and grinned. 'Whatever, I reckon you're a match for him this year.'

Just then Geraldine appeared wearing a big grin. 'Hi James, how are you today?' She kissed him on the cheek and Mugsy gave a big wink as James wiped it off, somewhat discomfited.

'What are you so pleased about?' he asked Geraldine.

'That's my uncle I was talking to, we're all staying in our usual houses for the duration of the regatta, and we've joined forces so we can enter more competitions. The "Surrey Superstars", we're calling ourselves, we've had T-shirts printed. Look,' she stretched her t-shirt out.

'Nice,' said Mugsy.

'Very nice, very nice indeed,' cut in Alex, who had just appeared, 'I'm going to make it three in a row, Smith,' he said to James, picking up three large stones and attempting unsuccessfully to juggle them; he dropped one on Bas's shin who yelped;

'Look what you're doing! I'm going to be in no fit state to row if you keep throwing rocks at me!'

Alex turned his attention back to James, 'do you think you can stop me this year? I just hope that your boat doesn't fall apart and sink half way across, it looks as if it could do that if some thing hard hit it - like a salmon perhaps.'

Bas laughed raucously in appreciation and Alex grinned at him, then the pair turned away towards their own boat.

'You were saying, Gerry?' James turned back to her, 'when you were so rudely interrupted.' He stared at Alex's retreating back, what was he supposed to have done to earn his dislike? They had been reasonably friendly until the last year of primary school and it wasn't that long ago he had been invited to Alex's birthday party at the Victoria hall. Or perhaps it was... he remembered they'd had balloons and jelly and played pass the parcel...

'I'm going to go out in my uncle's cruiser; he's going to follow the race so I'll be able to cheer you on. It's called the "Milly Bee," he launched her last night at Polly steps. He's got a temporary mooring on that side of the Salty. It's a beauty, massive Mercury engine, he's promised to take me water-skiing later on in the regatta.'

'I didn't know you were into water-skiing.'

'I'm not, but the weather's so beautiful and he's got a boat and water skis, so I thought I'd give it a try.'

'I'd like a wet-bike,' said Mugsy wistfully, 'but my dad won't even discuss it; anyway, don't we need to get going, or we'll miss the tow to Dawlish breakwater.'

They strode to the Lucy Ann, which been beached a few yards above tide level after their morning row. There was a frantic melee as people launched their dinghies into the water, whilst others pulled them down the beach over the sand.

'It's warm this year,' said James, 'the sea is warm as well. We went to Italy last year and this is just like the Mediterranean.' The clear water gently broke over his feet. He stood for a few moments enjoying the sensation and looked at the array of boats. A crab gently nibbled his toes.

Mugsy jumped in first and took his position whilst James pushed the boat into the swell and jumped in himself. The pair settled themselves, then rowed a few yards from the beach so they had more room to check everything was in order.

'Lifejackets!' shouted Geraldine. James scrabbled in the locker to retrieve his, and passed Mugsy's to him. He zipped it up and fastened the strap.

'I'm ready.'

'So am I,' panted Mugsy, 'but I think my life jacket has shrunk.'

'I said you'd put on weight… I mean muscle,' smiled James.

'There's the tow boat,' Mugsy pointed to a small open motorboat hovering well clear of the shore.

James nodded, 'yes, I can see it. Just a minute while I put my trainers on.' He had slung them round his neck to keep them out of the water. He removed them, untied the laces and slipped them on, crouching low to retie them.

'Ok I'm ready now, let's row over to our lift shall we?'

They reached the tow boat, signalling they were ready, one of the men nodded and gestured they would be second in line behind the "Esperanto."

'Our race is the fifth isn't it?' asked Mugsy.

James fished in his pocket and dug out a dog-eared and damp copy of the Regatta programme.

'Yes, fifth out of eight. Let's get hooked up, we're supposed to leave at 4.30.'

To observers on the Ness, the procession of dinghies each tied to the one in front, that followed the five tow boats, looked like an Aylesbury duck leading her chicks. The boats were strung out with sparkling waves splashing from each bow, the clearest sign they were moving. The sea was a deep blue, as the little knots made steady progress across the bay, heading towards Dawlish breakwater, out of sight to observers on the land at Teignmouth, shielded by Holcombe, a headland of reds cliffs between the two resorts. The lead boats skirted Teignmouth beach and headed beyond the pier, keeping to the seaward side of the string of yellow buoys marking the line separating craft and swimmers.

Several dinghies, out for a long recreational row to take advantage of the proximity of safety boats, laboured behind the oarsmen and women, sweating in the fierce heart of the afternoon, tempered a little by a fitful breeze. A yacht came close by, its sails flapping as the helmsman tried to catch the wind. Motor boats of all shapes and sizes swept past them, full of spectators.

'Go for it Lucy Ann!' someone shouted, James looked up and waved to Geraldine who waved wildly back.

***

The first competition started shortly after 5.30. Eventually the bunches of dinghies clustered round the breakwater disappeared, as their respective races were called, until at last the contestants for the Leander cup were called.

'Youngsters only, don't forget,' shouted the starter, 'we don't want any oldies in this one. There are five dinghies entered, make yourselves known and look lively,' he put a megaphone to his mouth and bellowed, 'give them some room, please,' at a little group of spectator boats, that motored to a more respectful distance.

'Boat 1, Lucy Ann - James Smith and Malcolm Adler.' James laughed as he always did on hearing Mugsy's real name. Geraldine heard as well and made a face, making him laugh even more. He bent to reset the footrest down a notch and made himself comfortable. Mugsy settled into a slightly different position, and grasped his oar firmly.

'…And boat number 5 is the "Redoubtable" with Barry Masters and Alexander Johnson, that's it, lads, get in position, behind the line please, yes the one painted on the surface of the water number 4. You all know the rules, so be aware of other vessels or swimmers, particularly as you enter the harbour. The tide is running fairly strongly, or it will be by the time you get there… we've got an excellent safety record and we don't intend to lose it. Most of all don't crash into any of the clay ships, we don't want you to damage them.'

There was a nervous ripple of laughter. 'In a line, Mr Masters, I haven't given the signal to start yet, draw back a few yards please.' Then the signal was given and the race began.

James and Mugsy rowed steadily at the number of strokes per minute agreed as part of their race plan. At first they fell back as their competitors rowed frantically. James stared ahead and pulled hard. It was a beautiful evening, the wind was light and there was virtually no swell. The fierce heat that had accompanied them on arrival had given way to a pleasant warmth. In previous years they had often rowed in fairly difficult conditions, facing choppy waves breaking over the bow or amidships, sometimes encountering a strong headwind from the Ness that made movement difficult. The organisers always had safety uppermost, they wouldn't hesitate to call off a race should adverse conditions warrant it.

James glanced at Mugsy, who was rowing strongly and rhythmically; thinking he must be much the same size as Bas this year, who had made all the difference between the crews in previous years, for he considered himself as good a rower as Alex himself.

'Row, row, stroke, stroke,' called James, 'we're slipping behind our race plan speed, we're going to get too far behind if we don't speed up.'

'Blow that,' said Mugsy, but he pulled harder on the next stroke, almost making James overbalance. The pier came into sight in the far distance, shimmering in the heat.

James felt it useful to detach mind from body when rowing. During one race he had concentrated on continually reciting the poem they had learnt in the spring term at school. What was the poem now?

"I must go down to the seas again to the lonely…"

'Pardon?' said Mugsy, 'did you say you want us to step up the pace?'

'No, it's OK, said James who had not realised he

had spoken aloud. This time he made sure he just thought the poem;

"I must go down to the seas again for the call of the turning tide

Is a wild call and a clear call that may not be denied

And all I ask is a windy day with the white clouds flying

And the flung spray and the blown spume and the seagulls crying"

He broke off, he wasn't sure if he would ever be able to feel the same about seagulls again, and wondered if anyone had ever written a poem about rowing. Gerry loved poems as much as he and his parents. He remembered what Mugsy had said last year when they had lost, and James had admitted he had become distracted through thinking of that poem.

Mugsy was scornful of poetry, indeed he had few literary bones in his body, maintaining steadfastly to his class teacher on one famous occasion that Dickens had written the Shakespeare sonnets.

James looked up to survey the route in front. The real skill -assuming you were still up with the leaders at that stage - was manoeuvring for position at the estuary mouth.

He scanned the sea. Where were the dolphins? He hadn't seen them for a few weeks now; there were often around six of them in the bay. The Ness glowed a soft red in the late sun and was nearing fast. It was time to start concentrating again. He tried to put his brain back in gear and said loudly:

'You OK, Mugsy?'

'Mmm… fine,' came the reply.

They were now parallel to the beach at Teignmouth. He could make out people swimming or standing in the waves, staring at them. Some waved.

The rapid pace of the race had exhausted some of the competitors and they were slipping back, causing the dinghies to become spread over a large area of sea.

James looked round quickly, there were three boats behind, he did another quick scan, where was the fifth boat? Ahead or behind?

He became aware of the spectator boats for the first time as he started to concentrate hard for the last part of the race. One came too close and they wobbled in its wake.

'Sorry!' came a voice.

'Keep clear, please!' yelled a race official from somewhere in the maze of boats. James could hear Geraldine calling, 'Lucy Ann, Lucy Ann!'

Where was the fifth boat – the one with Alex in? Ah, there it was, well to the left of them and just ahead.

Surely it had gone too far out towards the sea? Entering the estuary mouth at the correct angle and on the best side was a crucial part of the race, and this depended on the direction and strength of the wind, as well as the state of the tide.

'Keep this line, Mugsy, we can row with the tide - it'll sweep us in.'

'I know,' came an irritated voice, 'I have lived here all my life!'

James smiled. 'Pull, pull!' He spoke clearly as he upped the pace.

Mugsy responded immediately.

'Alex is well off to the side,' called James.

Mugsy looked up briefly. 'Wow! He's way over, he'll need to come right back over to our side, or his boat will be out of the current.'

'He's starting to pull over,' said James, 'he's too late I think. He won't be able to get across in time surely?'

The Lucy Ann was now well inside the estuary mouth and spectators on the Point at Teignmouth and standing on the beach road at Shaldon, were calling encouragement. A black Labrador and an Alsatian were splashing at the edge of the sand, barking excitedly.

'He's coming towards us now,' yelled James, 'he's veered right over!'

'He can't,' panted Mugsy, 'he'll hit us, he hasn't got the space to get through.'

The other boat was now heading directly towards them, the two rowers pulling hard, not seeming to see the Lucy Ann and its increasingly anxious occupants. There was a splash as the oars clashed and the boats bumped.

'Hey!' yelled James angrily, 'move over!'

The other boat had lost the momentum it had built up and the Lucy Ann emerged some two lengths clear, they were close to the beach and James heard another dog barking frantically.

'It's Einstein,' yelled Mugsy, 'and there are your mum and dad.' Mum was waving wildly at James.

'You're clear of them, just keep going,' she shouted. Einstein barked her agreement.

The finishing flag appeared in view fluttering gently on the Shaldon beach and he got a glimpse of the other boat being rowed frantically, but still well behind, as they both drew near to the finish point.

The commentator described the last few moments over the Tannoy;

'The Lucy Ann is maintaining the lead that it gained when it took a better line coming into the estuary, she's passing over the line... now! The Redoubtable is some three lengths behind, and is passing the line... now!'

There were some loud cheers from the crowd. 'First is Lucy Ann rowed by James Smith and Malcolm Adler, second is...'

The pair rowed slowly to the beach, Mr Smith appeared, grabbed the prow and pulled the boat up the beach a little.

'Well done! Well done, you two! That was nicely judged. I thought they were going to sink you when they came across like that, they were taking completely the wrong line as they came in to the estuary weren't they?'

Alex drew up his boat right next to the Lucy Ann, almost falling into the water as he scrambled out in a fury.

'Smith, you cheat!' He yelled, 'you tried to ram us! What the hell do you think you were doing? Couldn't bear the idea of losing, could you?'

'It wasn't me,' said James in surprise, 'you came across us, you hit us - not the other way round.'

'It's true, Alex,' said Mr Smith quietly, 'I don't think you saw them, but you were on completely the wrong line as you came in. You hit them'

Alex looked angrily at him, 'We'll see about all that!' With that he splashed across to the umpire's boat, waving at them frantically to catch their attention. He could be heard yelling angrily as the umpire looked on impassively, then shook his head. Alex started yelling again, the umpire shook his head again and turned away, the conversation as far as he was concerned being at an end.

'What a cheek,' said Mr Smith, 'everyone could see he wasn't looking, he crashed into you, not the other way round.'

'It seems the umpire agrees,' said Mugsy as the umpire boat reversed into the channel and motored off to oversee the next race.

Geraldine's boat arrived just off the beach and she jumped into the water and waded ashore.

'James! Well done,' she said throwing her arms round him and kissed him on the cheek for the second time that day. Then she turned to Mugsy, 'well done! You were wonderful.'

'Thanks, Gerry,' murmured Mugsy, 'I wish other people were as happy.' He nodded behind them. Alex came splashing back to his boat, which Bas was holding steady in the shallows, looking somewhat sheepish.

'I'll get you, Smith, see if I don't, stop at nothing to look good in front of your girlfriend won't you,' Alex shouted

'She's not my girlfriend and it was your fault... you weren't looking, you were way out of position and tried to come across too sharply. I keep telling you and so does everyone else.'

Alex pushed the boat out and jumped in. 'Come on, Bas, there's a nasty smell here, let's row somewhere where the air is a bit fresher.'

James looked at their disappearing boat in dismay.

'Never mind, James,' said Gerry, 'you and Mugsy were mega brilliant.'

'Are you going to stay around for the presentation?' asked Mr Smith.

'I might as well,' said James, 'there's still some other races to go, but I guess they'll be handing out the trophies in an hour or perhaps less. We'll draw the boat up and watch the finish of the other races. Steve and Darren are in one of them, it'd be nice to see how they get on.'

'Do you want some fish and chips?' asked his dad, 'then we can sit on the beach and watch the last few races. I'll stroll up to George's, if we get there now we should be ahead of the rush. Geraldine and Mugsy, would you like some? If I have to get Einstein a sausage it seems unreasonable not to get food for you as well.'

'Yes, please,' they both echoed; Mr Smith turned away.

Mugsy threaded his way through the crowds on the beach, which seemed to be thinning a bit, and returned with the roller. Some spectators helped to draw the Lucy Ann back up to its spot just below the Ferry Boat Inn. Geraldine rolled up the ramp and went off to put it back in its proper place.

James scrabbled under the dinghy to put the upturned keel back on to the brick that kept it just off the sand.

'What's this?'

'What's what? asked Mugsy, who was holding the boat steady as James scrabbled around underneath.

'It's a piece of wood,' he brought it out and shook the sand off, 'no, it seems to be a bit of metal, it's a bit strange, it feels a bit warm.

'It's been lying half buried in the sand,' said Geraldine who had just returned, 'it's bound to be warm.'

'It's silver... the material's very peculiar. It's sort of L-shaped, quite fat, look what do you think it is?'

Mugsy took the object and looked at it casually, 'it could be a bit off an engine,' he said a little doubtfully, '...off an outboard engine perhaps, they tend to have lots of strange shaped bits that are always falling off.'

Geraldine took it from Mugsy, looked at it, handed it back to James and shrugged, 'it looks like something off a barbecue.'

'I'll put it in the rubbish bin later,' said James and slipped it in his pocket, and then they all trudged off the beach towards the Clipper, where mum was standing waving from the access that led from the Strand, with Einstein sitting at her feet looking at James, her tail wagging furiously.

'Well done, James!'

'Thanks, mum.'

'And you, Mugsy, you looked really sturdy out there, I remember how skinny you used to be when you...'

'Oh, mum,' cut in James embarrassed, 'no-one's interested in all our baby stuff, or what we did when we were five or something.'

'I am,' said Geraldine.

'How lovely to see you again, Geraldine. My word, you've grown up since last year! Women are more interested in memories,' agreed mum, 'men are so insensitive, anyway, what was all that bumping as you came into the estuary, it looked as if Alex was trying to run you down?'

'Not you as well' sighed James, 'it was an accident, he just wasn't looking.'

'Hmm,' said mum, 'it didn't look that way to me. Ah, there's dad,' she continued, 'hey, we're over here!'

She waved as Einstein leapt up at him barking frantically. 'You were a long time, I hope you've got her sausage or you'll be torn limb from limb.'

'The chip shop was packed,' said dad, 'the queue was down the street,' and then as an afterthought, 'and if she tears me limb from limb she won't get her sausage, tell her to think on that.'

'She'll get fresh meat though,' said James, 'she might prefer that.' They walked to the quay and sat on its edge. Einstein started barking again and pulled furiously.

'It's those wretched seagulls over there,' said mum, 'they drive this dog mad, 'gulls can be a real nuisance, and they seem so aggressive this year.'

'I don't know what she'd do with it if she actually caught one,' said dad, 'the trouble is the visitors feed them. I wish they wouldn't.'

James tried to get comfortable on the stone, there was something sticking through his shorts and in to his leg. He pulled the item from his pocket and glanced up.

The Duck Man was on the edge of the crowd close by, 'Ducks, get your lovely ducks here, buy your winner for the great duck race,' he caught James' glance and turned away.

Einstein continued growling. There were two seagulls just in front of them, grey with brown speckled heads. One pulled at a worm in the wet sand, whilst the other stood on one leg and drummed on a pebble with the other.

James glanced at the object; it felt very warm in his hand. 'Of course,' he said softly to himself, 'it's the key.'

Chapter Four

THE new Duck Man had moved to the village last summer. He lived in a flat with his wife above the haberdasher's shop he had opened adjacent to the estate agent.

James had only the vaguest idea as to what such shops sold. There was cotton and wool and knitting patterns in the window, which he had glanced at contemptuously. Clearly there must be more to the shop than met the eye, even adults couldn't possibly be interested in such items, bizarre as their tastes might be, seeming to find great interest in such tedious things as old buildings and views.

He had been disappointed by the appearance of the haberdashers, as there had been a strong rumour flying round the younger residents of Shaldon that it was going to be a chocolate shop. A haberdasher was beneath the contempt of a 13-year-old boy, so consequently he had dismissed it from his mind.

He walked past it on his way to the bakers, altogether a much more interesting store. Mum had made him some sandwiches as he had arranged to meet the others at 11 for what was termed in the programme as 'Happy-go-lucky water sports.' James was a good swimmer but there were lots of better ones in the village. Alex for one. Mugsy could swim to the shore if a boat capsized, but was neither stylish nor fast. So consequently neither of them were entering. Geraldine, though...

James pushed open the narrow door to the bakers. There was one person ahead of him. They bought some bread and two Danish pastries and left.

'Hello, James,' smiled the assistant, 'how are you this morning?'

'Hi, yes, fine thank you. Can I have three doughnuts and three Eccles cakes, please, and a cheese and onion pasty and two steak and kidney pies?'

'Hungry, are you today, James?'

'Oh, no, it's not all for me,' he explained hastily as the assistant grinned. 'I'm meeting up with two of my friends.'

'I believe you,' the woman put the items into paper bags which James placed into his rucksack. 'Are you in the swimming, that's today isn't it?'

'Not me, but Geraldine - my friend - is entered in the last one, "Girls not yet 15." I think she said her dad was also entering.'

'Not in the girls not yet 15 race though, I expect? Or are the rules quite flexible?'

James smiled, 'I shouldn't think so. Gerry's an ace swimmer, though, she swims in her youth team in Surrey where she lives, they all come up for the regatta every year.'

'Yes I'm sure I've seen her with you and Malcolm.' James nodded and went out the door as the next customer entered. He looked left to see if Mugsy should happen to be walking that way towards their meeting place from his home in Ringmore. He wasn't in sight so James turned right towards the river beach.

As he passed the haberdasher's shop he noticed something on the ground. He picked it up - some sort of bottle top or something, he thought vaguely. He rammed it in his pocket intending to put it in a rubbish bin and crossed the road. An open-top car passed along and he swivelled round to watch its progress. The Duck Man was framed in the doorway of his shop and seemed to be shouting something at him, which was lost in the noise from the car. James shivered and hastened on, there was something distinctly odd about that man's behaviour. He strode on past the Clipper café where he and his friends tended to congregate in the winter when the Beachcomber was shut.

He turned down the little alley that led to the beach, sat on one of the concrete bollards and pulled the programme from his pocket. "Beach volleyball at 2pm." The Surrey Superstars were entered in that. Stupid name, but all the visitor's teams seemed to be going in for daft names. Many of them had even gone to the trouble of having t-shirts printed with their team names emblazoned on them. He must meet up with the others and have a council of war about the boy, and Digger and Drum, and the Duck Man, who always seemed to be there when something untoward was happening. They must also talk about the key as well. But when? Today would be busy.

What time was it now? He glanced at his watch, just before 11... high tide. He scrutinised the programme again 'Oh, no!' he said aloud, he scratched his head and stood up.

It wasn't the water sports and volleyball at all, that was tomorrow- Tuesday. It was just the rounders today. "Under 14's - to be played under Shaldon rules". He smiled, when the venue was a narrow beach with the village on one side and the sea on the other, Shaldon rules had to cater for every eventuality, mostly revolving round balls being frequently hit into the water.

Geraldine might have said she was intending to enter that. Still, that was good, as it would leave most of the day free. He looked at his programme again - 2pm start, well that would make sense, there would be no point in having rounders at high tide when there wasn't much of a beach left. The collectors in the boat would be forever retrieving balls from the river.

'Gerry must have misread the programme,' he said aloud to no one in particular, 'she definitely said there was volleyball on today.'

He patted the key, which was wrapped in a handkerchief in his pocket. Where were Digger and Drum at the moment? The two seagulls had been sitting on the balcony rail looking into the living room when he had come down for breakfast that morning, but they had fluttered away to sit in the cherry tree when Einstein had rushed at the patio doors towards them, barking furiously.

'Sorry, James,' said Geraldine with a grimace as he turned into the Beachcomber garden. She was sitting on one of the chairs at the series of tables that fronted the wall that afforded some of the best views of the beach, the estuary, and Teignmouth. The umbrellas were erected to shade them from the hot sun. Even at this time of day it was strong enough to be uncomfortable, but was tempered by a slight breeze travelling from the sea.

'Sorry?' James queried.

'I mixed up the programme big time.' She touched his hand and James withdrew it hastily.

'Oh, that. It's OK, I realised. I've had time to get over my huge disappointment.'

'I'm playing in the rounders today at 2, it's tomorrow I'm going to be occupied virtually all day playing in various games, as the undisputed top athlete of the Surrey Superstars.'

James nodded, 'where's Mugsy, is he here yet?'

'Here,' came a voice, as Mugsy collapsed into the spare chair panting. 'I've run all the way from home as I didn't want to be late and incur the displeasure of you two.'

'Sorry, Mugsy,' said Geraldine sweetly, 'you've run all this way for nothing. I screwed up I'm afraid. It was too late to phone you as I only realised when I got here just now and realised the state of the tide. Just pretend it's Tuesday.'

'Pardon?' said Mugsy. 'What are you talking about? Have I missed something?'

'Wrong day,' said James, 'it could be worse it could be the wrong month. Or even the wrong year. Still, I'm glad I've got you two here, we need to have a chat.'

'Boys don't chat, said Geraldine scornfully, 'they talk earnestly about things they think are important like computer games and football, they gossip worse than women, and often they don't say anything at all... but chat? Never.'

'Anyway,' said James somewhat taken aback by Geraldine's insight into males, 'some strange things have been happening ever since that boy first appeared.'

'That poor boy who drowned? I didn't think you knew him, I thought he was a visitor.'

'I didn't know him, but I did speak to him twice.'

'Has his body been found?' cut in Geraldine.

'No, not yet, the tide must have swept it to Newton Abbot as it was flowing in quite strongly. But there have been a lot of strong tides since, so it's probably been swept out again to sea by now... it'll land up in Exmouth.'

'Yuk!' said Geraldine, 'how terrible.'

'He'd approached some other boys before he spoke to me, the previous evening I think.'

'The previous afternoon, it was,' remarked Mugsy, 'you remember me saying Alex and his friends had been showing off at the quay by jumping in to the river?'

'They always do that,' said Geraldine, 'whenever it's warm, let's hope they bother to look to see if the tide is in before they jump.'

'Anyway,' continued Mugsy, 'I'd been there as well and when Alex had finished jeering at him he came over to me. I was sitting on one of those benches by the slipway. Anyway, the boy had told me much the same story that you did. That we'd soon be following in the footsteps of the Egyptians and the Hippopotamus...'

Geraldine looked mystified. 'Hippopotamus? Why would he talk about them?'

'Mesopotamia,' said James, 'the cities of Mesopotamia, not Hippopotamus.'

'Same difference,' continued Mugsy unperturbed, 'then he carried on about the Romans. 1066, that was, wasn't it, when Nero conquered us?'

'Mugsy!' said Geraldine in exasperation, 'you're making this bit up, even you aren't that hopeless at history.'

'History and English are my weak points,' admitted Mugsy, 'apart from that I'm virtually perfect.'

James broke in, 'that's all by the by. The boy had been around for two or three nights then, before he drowned, he must have been a visitor or he would have been recognised by someone living here. I'd never seen him before. If he was from Shaldon we would have known him, if he'd been from Teignmouth we would at least have recognised him. He must have come from out of the area.'

'So where had he been staying whilst he was here?' asked Gerry.

'No one knows, no one has come forward, and I hadn't seen him around before that time I saw him on the beach.'

'Why would he approach Alex at all?'

'Same age, perhaps,' said James, 'he looked around thirteen or fourteen, perhaps he felt he'd rather confide in someone his own age rather than an adult who would probably try to lock him up as mad. Perhaps he doesn't trust adults because of the Duck Man.'

'The Duck Man,' said Geraldine in surprise, 'who, him?' She nodded towards the Duck Man as he came into the café garden and approached some visitors with his clipboard, asking if they'd like to select a duck.

'Yes, shhh! Wait until he's gone.'

The Duck Man put the money from the visitors in his pouch and walked past the table where the three friends were sat, then stepped out of the gate and onto the beach.

'Oh!' said Geraldine, 'what have you done to upset him, James?'

'What do you mean,' he asked nervously.

'If looks could kill... you should have seen the glare he gave you. Anyway, carry on.'

'Well, the boy said he was being pursued by those seagulls -mechanicals, he called them. He said he'd prove it if I promised to meet him at sunset. So he just jumped up and dashed into the sea.'

'So that's when he drowned then,' cut in Geraldine.

'Will you let me finish, Gerry? Just like a female to keep interrupting.' Mugsy grinned as Geraldine blew an exaggerated mock kiss and said:

'Continue, I shall not utter another word – ever.'

'He was chased by the seagulls… definitely chased by them, and he came back and sat on the beach with the seagulls just… well… just strutting around as if they were standing guard over him. That evening I saw him again because I'd promised. Mugsy was with me.' Mugsy nodded his agreement.

James continued. 'That's when he said much the same to me as he'd said to Alex, he talked about Romans and Egyptians and about Mugsy's Hippos, and then he said… you're next, not me personally, of course, it wasn't in that context, but our civilisation, and he talked of the Watchers on the rocks and Guardians and a key that the Guardians needed in order to get in. He wanted to give it to me as he said they'd soon get him, he wouldn't just hand it direct to me though, as he said the seagulls would attack me. I told him to leave it under the boat. It was then he saw the Duck Man and was obviously terrified of him.'

'That's true,' said Mugsy, 'he said it's one of the Watchers.'

'That's right,' agreed James, 'and then the boy got up and ran off to hide in the crowd, but the Duck Man seemed to try to head him off and the seagulls flew into the air as if to mark where he was. That was when the boy just ran towards the river and dived in trying to escape them. The tide was coming in very strongly and he just disappeared…'

'And the seagulls? asked Mugsy 'I didn't see what happened to them.'

'They flew down the estuary to the Ness,' said James.

Geraldine was waving furiously. 'Can I talk now?'

James smiled, 'I suppose, although I thought you had taken a vow of silence?

'I'm hoping to become a politician,' said Geraldine sweetly, 'so my vows mean absolutely nothing.'

'What was it you wanted to say?' asked James, 'as you are now officially released from the vows you didn't intend to keep anyway.'

'The boy sounds mad. He was just an unfortunate person who had an obsession with seagulls. Perhaps they were following him because he'd been cruel to them or his shirt smelt of fish. Virtually calling them jailers and saying they were stalking him seems rather far fetched.'

'You weren't there,' said James quietly.

'I know, but talk of mechanical seagulls, Watchers, Romans… there's no sense to any of it.'

'I agree with Gerry,' said Mugsy, 'sometimes people just do very strange things and it becomes such an obsession they need help for it. Do you remember my Uncle John? He needed therapy when he became convinced his boss was trying to get him sacked. They were really good to him, but in the end it became a sort of self fulfilling prophecy, perhaps the boy really believed seagulls were after him… maybe if one of them just looked at him he became steadily madder until he lost all reason.'

'Well I've been thinking hard about it,' said James, 'and until last night I would have been inclined to dismiss it all, I'd even thought the same as Gerry, that his clothes had become tainted with fish smells and they were after him because of that. But when we drew up the Lucy Ann on to her mooring last night, do you remember I found this underneath it?'

He fumbled in his pocket and drew out an object that he placed on the table.

'Yuk,' said Geraldine for the second time that morning, 'that didn't use to be a handkerchief in a past life did it? It looks disgusting.'

James unwrapped the item. 'It's the key, the boy disappeared in the crowd when he saw the Duck Man but he must have had time to leave it under the Lucy Ann.'

Mugsy looked at it doubtfully, 'was that the thing you showed us yesterday? In all the excitement of our great win I didn't look very closely at it? Hmmm… doesn't look much like a key to me, more like an outboard engine part. Now I've looked more closely at it that's still what I think.'

'To me it still looks a bit like the little handle you have on a barbecue only rather fatter,' said Geraldine, 'you know the bit that goes on the spit thing you're supposed to roast chickens on, not that I've seen anyone ever using the spit.'

'Pick it up,' said James, 'then look behind you at the front wall.' Geraldine picked it up gingerly, conspicuously trying to avoid touching the handkerchief.

'Hmm, it's surprisingly heavy and I don't recognise the metal it's made out of.'

She passed it to Mugsy, who felt it and commented 'it feels warm,' before handing it back to Geraldine who said:

'Where am I supposed to look? The front wall, did you say?'

'Yes, what do you see?'

'Hmm,' said Geraldine, 'some Geraniums that need watering, a bicycle... oh, and two seagulls. This is a seaside village, James, it's stuffed full of seagulls, you know. Mostly giant ones. Perhaps people ought to start eating them to reduce the numbers.'

'Seagull and chips,' murmured Mugsy.

'Seagull pasties,' giggled Geraldine, 'oops, sorry James,' she said hastily when she caught sight of his face. 'It's two seagulls lurking, so what?'

'What colour are they?' asked James.

'Grey, with brown speckled heads.'

'And what are they doing?'

'They're juggling. Sorry, sorry, but they're doing seagullish type things. One is trying to pull out a worm and the other seems to be bashing its leg against a stone.'

'Digger and Drum. They follow the key.'

Geraldine looked at the two birds curiously, 'why did you give them such strange names?'

'I didn't, it's what the stranger called them.'

She stared hard at the birds again. 'I think we should stop calling him the boy, or the visitor or the stranger, can we give him a name? It sounds more respectful, something simple... what about Adam?'

'That's sounds fine,' agreed James.

Geraldine continued, 'Why do you call them mechanicals... as in robots? They look exactly like ordinary seagulls, you know. Doing ordinary seagull things. They're not doing anything mysterious. Are you sure its not you that's becoming obsessed?'

'Mechanicals are what Adam called them; it was one of the first things he said to me. There's six of them in total, the other four seem to appear only when they are needed... sort of reinforcements I guess. We've got a few hours spare,' continued James, 'as a certain person lured us here on false pretences.'

Geraldine blushed, 'It's the programme,' she protested, 'they should have made the information clearer. Larger type... and some sort of audio facility that speaks the days,' she continued straight-faced.

'So it's not your fault then?' said James grinning, 'we've got some food, can we go and look for the Watchers on the Rocks?'

'The Watchers watched, that sounds a good title for a poem.'

'Oh, no,' Mugsy groaned, 'it's bad enough with him spouting poetry, have I ever mentioned we lost the race last year because he was trying to write a poem whilst we were rowing?'

'Lots of times,' said Geraldine firmly. She turned to James, 'where do you want to look?'

'The Ness, that's what he was staring at. It's all connected with the Ness.'

'Ok,' agreed Mugsy, 'it's a nice day for a picnic.'

James picked up the key and stretched a hand towards the handkerchief.

'You're not going to put that key thing back in that... that object,' said Geraldine pointedly, ' My theory is that the Watchers are probably health and safety people keeping a look out for your handkerchief.' James looked blankly at her.

'It's not that bad, it's only a handkerchief.'

'No doubt at one time it used to be a handkerchief,' said Geraldine, 'it's probably metamorphosed into a new life form by now.'

'Hold on,' said Mugsy, he stood up and plunged his hand in his pocket. 'Here why not wrap it in this, it'll stop it poking into your leg.'

'What is it?' asked Geraldine, 'it looks like lead, but no sane person goes round with lead in their pocket.'

'It is lead,' agreed Mugsy. 'I got it for the oars, they weren't balanced very well, they're building an extension on our house and need lead to join it on to the main house. The builder said it stops the water getting in, flashing, he called it. I asked if I could have a bit. He didn't realise what it was for,' he finished in glee, 'or he wouldn't have given it to me as his son was rowing in the same race as us!'

'Do you mean Benji?' said James nervously, 'I hope he never finds out, he's a giant.'

'Anyway, there it is, use it if you want,' concluded Mugsy putting it down on the tabletop. James placed the key in the middle and folded the soft metal round it like a pie crust, then picked up the handkerchief and absentmindedly stuffed it in his pocket.

***

They trudged along the beach towards the Ness, then onto the adjacent road, as the tide was too full to walk alongside the water. 'Curious things, tides,' mused James, 'most visitors just think a tide is a tide.'

'That's profound,' said Geraldine, 'but I don't know what you mean.'

'Well, they just think the water level is always fairly constant. There was that family last year we saw in the Teignmouth tourist information office complaining the sand had disappeared since they had been on the beach a few days previously. The woman tried to explain that the height of the tides varies day by day and the times they come in and out varies every day as well. She told them about spring tides and neap tides and how with spring tides you get high high tides and low low tides and neap tides produce low high tides and high low tides so there's not a lot of difference between them.'

'You don't intend to be a teacher do you?' asked Geraldine. 'You're starting to sound like my science teacher. I don't understand a word he says. I thought I knew all about tides already but I'm not sure I do any more after your explanation. Anyway, tides aren't an easy concept to understand,' she continued scathingly, 'especially if you don't come into contact with them very often. If you live up country and inland, tides must seem like an alien concept. It must be like trying to explain cricket to an American.'

'Or a woman,' murmured Mugsy.

'If you'd like to explain the LBW rule to me,' said Geraldine grinning, 'then afterwards I'll give you the correct definition.'

'Mugsy hates being out LBW,' agreed James, 'he just doesn't understand the concept of being out if he hasn't been bowled or caught. He thinks if he glares at the umpire they won't dare to give him out.'

'I read somewhere that Julius Caesar nearly didn't land in Britain as the Romans couldn't understand the idea of tides, coming from the Mediterranean where there aren't any to speak of.'

'He should have had a tide table,' said Mugsy unsympathetically, 'Anyway where do you want to look?'

'If we walk up to the top of the Ness first and have a look,' said James, 'and then perhaps we can go through the tunnel and on to the Ness beach, and if possible round the rocks and back to here. The tide's too high to do that just yet but we'll be able to do it in another half hour or so. That will mean we will have had a really good search for the Watchers.'

They walked up the footpath next to the sea that wound up in front of the Ness House Hotel, then continued up the hill and through the trees towards the viewpoint at the top, that had a panoramic view of Lyme Bay.

'Wait a minute, let's backtrack a little and go along the path that leads through the woods and away from the viewpoint first,' said James, 'and then swing round to the left at the bottom and come back up on the main path. Then we will have covered virtually the whole of the area.' They walked slowly, scanning the undergrowth.

After a few minutes Geraldine said, 'what exactly are we looking for? I've no idea so I might have missed hundreds of clues.'

'I don't know either,' said James truthfully, 'perhaps the Watchers are like bird-watchers, there might be a rucksack or a thermos flask that they have left behind.'

'Or a notebook,' said Mugsy, 'and a pen so they could take notes, and perhaps a copy of The Bird Watchers' Times.'

'And binoculars,' said Geraldine, 'you can't watch something unless you've got binoculars.'

'Yes, agreed James, 'all those things, they might have had sandwiches or crisps and discarded the wrappings, we need to look out for anything that's lying around that's not undergrowth or trees.' They came to the end of the path.

'Listen to that racket,' said Geraldine, 'it must scare visitors who don't know the zoo is there - must be feeding time.'

'It's the monkeys,' explained James, 'they're the worst for making noise, the zoo has got some new ones this year, we can hear them from our house. When we have visitors and they ask what the noise is you ought to see their faces when we explain it's monkeys.'

They turned left to go back up the main path, this time with the sea immediately to their right. They reached the top and sat down on the seat overlooking the viewpoint.

'Nothing,' said Geraldine, 'nothing at all out of the ordinary, unless you count an empty cigarette packet.'

'No,' agreed James reluctantly, 'and that looks as if it's been there for ages, it didn't have those huge warnings they have to have now.' They stared out to sea. Something was troubling James, but he couldn't put his finger on it. The tide was flowing out strongly.

'Shall we eat?' asked Mugsy, 'I'm starving.'

'There's a picnic table just below us, isn't there?' said Geraldine, 'we need to go in that direction anyway if we're going to do a full circuit.'

The three strode down the path back towards the Ness House Hotel and came to the picnic bench set just off the track, its top scarred by the heat from a portable barbecue.

They sat down and James swung the rucksack off his back and placed it at his feet. He undid the clasps and put the various packages on the bench.

'There's a cheese and onion pasty for you, Geraldine, I assume you're still vegetarian?'

'Is the Pope a Catholic?' she replied cheerfully.

'Don't ask me,' said Mugsy, 'I'm not religious.'

'Mugsy, steak and kidney pie for you?'

'Great, thanks.'

'And I've got some cheese sandwiches you're welcome to share, and there are some cakes as well.'

'Any drink?' asked Mugsy.

'I've got a bottle of diluted orange squash. I think it's very weak, I'm afraid, mum likes it like that and assumes everyone else must as well.' He rummaged in the rucksack, 'yes, here it is.' Mugsy took it, unscrewed the cap and took three big gulps.

'It's alright,' said Geraldine patiently, 'no one else wanted any.'

'Sorry,' said Mugsy sheepishly, wiping his mouth and handing the bottle to Geraldine.

James said. 'I've got a handkerchief if you want to wipe... Ouch, something's jabbing into my leg.'

'Probably a panther escaped from Shaldon zoo,' said Geraldine.

'They don't have panthers,' objected Mugsy, 'you'd have to go to Paignton Zoo for those. Although whenever I go there all the animals seem to hide from me. Perhaps they haven't really got any animals at all.'

James plunged his hand into his pocket and put the

object down on the table and looked at it in some bemusement.

'What on earth? Oh, yes, I think it's a bottle cap. I picked it up in the street this morning. Outside the Haberdashers that the Duck man runs.'

'Is this a new hobby, James?' asked Geraldine examining it, 'if so it's rather a disturbing one. 13-year-olds don't generally collect this sort of thing.'

'Hobby? Oh, no, nothing like that, I was going to put it in the bin but I forgot. What is it then?'

'Trust a boy not to know. Mugsy carries great lumps of roofing lead on him and you've got a thimble. Have you suddenly become domesticated? Is it going to be the ironing next?'

'Of course not,' James slipped the object back in his pocket. 'Ah! I knew I'd been feeling vaguely that something was wrong, but I couldn't think what. Now I know, where are Digger and Drum?' They always stay near by but I haven't seen them since we left the Beachcomber. That reminds me, is the key safe? I passed it over to you after we left the café.'

Mugsy felt in his pocket and drew out the piece of lead, which he unwrapped. 'Yes, it's OK.' He picked it up. 'It's feeling cold today.' James held out his hand and Mugsy tipped the key into it.

'I still think it's a handle for a barbecue,' said Geraldine.

'Or an engine part, confirmed Mugsy, 'you can't say the word outboard engine without a part dropping off it.'

'I thought you said it was cold?' said James.

'It was. Is.'

'It's not now, it's warm, it's getting very warm.'

'Look over there,' said Geraldine, 'on the fence, they obviously know it's lunch time.'

'Who?'

'Those two seagulls perched on the fence.'

James looked up; one bird was pulling at a loose wire strand that was poking up, whilst the other danced up and down. 'Digger and Drum! Where have they sprung from? They weren't around a few seconds ago.'

'Hold on,' said Geraldine reasonably, 'there must be lots of seagulls going round in pairs, it's what seagulls do.'

'I've got an idea,' said James, 'I'm going to take the key and walk down the path to the Ness House Hotel. I'll be back in a minute or two.' He disappeared and the seagulls flew into the air, wheeled over the sea and went from sight. James reappeared after a few minutes.

'You didn't get any crisps whilst you were at the Ness House, did you?' asked Mugsy hopefully.

'Of course I didn't. They followed me and perched on that bench near the telescope, looking hard at me.'

'Where are they now?' asked Geraldine.

'Cheese and onion or smoky bacon, I don't mind.'

'I can't see... oh, here they are,' said James, as the two birds reappeared and resumed their place on the fence.

'Roast chicken is quite nice but it tastes a bit like...'

'Mugsy, will you stop thinking about your stomach for a millisecond and take the key?'

'Me? Why?'

'Yours is not to reason why, yours is just to do and die,' murmured Geraldine.

'Ignore her, she's just showing off, now just take the key.'

Mugsy picked it up. 'Ow, it's hot.'

'Now walk down to the hotel and come back.'

Mugsy stared at him in bemusement for a moment then shrugged and set off. He reappeared after a few minutes panting and eating a bag of crisps. 'They only had ready salted, anyone want some? Phew! It's scorching out of the shade, you'll fry in the rounders competition this afternoon Gerry.'

'Did they follow you? They left the fence as soon as you started walking down the path.'

'Yes, they sat on the bench just outside the door when I went inside.'

'Geraldine, now you take the key, but I'm going to wrap it in this lead.'

'Why on earth..?' asked Geraldine mystified.

'He's been reading too many superman comics,' said Mugsy munching absent mindedly, 'he thinks the key is made of Kryptonite. That could be shielded by lead.'

'I never read any Superman comics,' said Geraldine. 'Gerry, just do it, will you, please?' pleaded James.

'Sure, I need the toilet anyway, see you in a few minutes.' Eventually she reappeared.

'They didn't move,' said Mugsy, 'they just stayed on the fence eyeing up my crisps. Roast seagull flavoured crisps, that would be a good one to sell in coastal towns.'

'It's the lead,' confirmed James, 'I don't know about Kryptonite but lead is used to shield things against radiation, and radio waves… all sorts of things. The stuff must be blocking whatever signal the key is emitting so the birds can't follow it.'

'Are you sure they weren't sticking around hoping that Mugsy was going to share his crisps with them? If they knew him though they would have realised they had no hope. Anyway, surely the key was lying under the boat before you found it, but the birds hadn't been hanging around or took it.'

'I don't know,' said James thoughtfully, 'perhaps someone actually has to be touching it before it transmits, or perhaps the sand was screening the signals.'

'It's nearly one o clock,' said Geraldine, 'if you hope to walk round the beach we need to do it now or I'll be late for the rounders.' They walked down the path towards the zoo, dropped down the steps that went past the toilets and entered the tunnel that led to the Ness beach.

It was said to be a smugglers tunnel as in the old days Ness cove would have been an attractive place to land contraband, being accessible to Shaldon and Teignmouth but hidden from them both by the great bulk of the headland.

'You can just imagine the smugglers,' said Geraldine, 'staggering along the passage to their hiding places with their barrels of brandy, after beaching their rowing boat at the cove and leaving a guard to keep an eye out for the revenue men. There's a poem about smuggling. Do you want to hear it?

'Oh, no,' said Mugsy in despair, 'he's bad enough, without you starting on as well.'

'You must have learnt it, Mugsy, it's very famous,' said Geraldine.

'I stopped being interested in poetry when I was forced to learn Hiawatha, that stuffed me so full of poems I didn't have room for any more. It's not

Hiawatha is it?' he asked anxiously, 'I don't remember anything about smuggling in it, but you lose the will to live after you reach the 1000th verse of Hiawatha.'

'No, it's not that one, but in the tunnel here is just the right place to recite the one I'm thinking of.' Mugsy reluctantly stopped and Geraldine began, her voice echoing.

"If you wake at midnight and hear a horses fee
Don't go drawing back the blind or looking in the street
Them that asks no questions isn't told a lie
Watch the wall my darling while the gentlemen go by."

Mugsy stared at the circle of light at the tunnel entrance as he stood and listened to Gerry. She had a good dramatic voice enhanced by the acoustics of the tunnel. It was quite a stirring poem and he tapped his fingers on the wall as she intoned;

Brandy for the parson
Baccy for the clerk…"

Although he would not have admitted it to anyone he was almost disappointed when Gerry triumphantly concluded;

"Them that asks no questions isn't told a lie
Watch the wall my darling while the gentlemen go by!"

'Hmm better than Hiawatha,' said Mugsy reluctantly, 'but only just,' he added hastily to forestall any further literary efforts.

'You missed out a few verses,' said James.

I know, I wanted to spare Mugsy dying from boredom, besides there were people listening.'

'One applauded,' said James, 'it's a shame we didn't put down a cap as people might have put money in it, it would pay for some of Mugsy's food bill.'

They dropped down a flight of steps, then another, and emerged blinking into the sunlight at the end of the tunnel, still fairly high above the Ness beach that was accessed by a further flight of steps. They clattered down them and turned left on to the sand.

'The beach café is just back there,' said Mugsy wistfully, 'we could get some cheesy chips. They're famous for it.'

'Yuk! Infamous more like. They're disgusting,' said Geraldine, 'really fatty and greasy.'

'That's their point,' said Mugsy in puzzlement, 'it makes them really tasty.'

At low tide it was possible to scramble round the rocks under the Ness and emerge onto the beach in front of the Ness House hotel, which in turn was a continuation of the main river beach. James stood for a moment perched on the first rocky outcrop, looking at the cliff face, still startlingly red no matter how often he looked at it.

'Come on,' said Geraldine, 'we'd better get a move on or I will be late.'

'Not too fast though,' cautioned Mugsy, 'I sprained my ankle here once.'

'The tides dropped,' pronounced James, 'we should be able to get right round without too much trouble.'

'At least it is still going out,' said Geraldine as she jumped from one rock to another, 'some people take a risk trying to get along here when the tide's coming in.'

The three friends cautiously picked their way round in a line abreast, looking for Watchers or their paraphernalia. The jumbled scatter of rocks gave way to smoother ones, worn flat by the sea.

The channel into the harbour lay immediately to their right, ringed by yellow buoys which marked the deep water. They looked so close to the shore that it seemed impossible that big ships could use the channel and enter the docks.

The tide was now flowing out strongly. James looked up at the face of the Ness which showed the aftermath of recent landslips, several dead trees lying at grotesque angles, grey branches pointing heavenwards, surrounded by red sand that had slipped off the cliff and not yet been reclaimed by the sea or crowned by plants. A cable sprang from the headland taking power to the floodlights that illuminated the Ness in the summer months. As they walked round, huge chunks of red sandstone at its base gave further testament to its steady erosion that accelerated in very wet, cold, or stormy weather.

'There's no sign of your Watchers James.'

James turned and stared out to sea then murmured thoughtfully, 'The tide was coming in when Adam dived into the water but the seagulls flew down river following something, not upriver where the current would have taken him. They flew just above the water, but going against the tide.'

'What are you saying?' asked Geraldine as they clambered over the last of the rocks and regained the beach.

'I saw something just before the boy disappeared and his body has not been found. Whatever happened, the birds were following something that was in the water, perhaps… perhaps something scooped him up. A submarine or something'

Geraldine looked at Mugsy who raised his eyebrows. She said softly, 'You're developing a bit of a conspiracy theory here, aren't you, James? Seagulls often fly low over the water, they might have been following a shoal of fish.'

'Sorry,' said James, 'I know it sounds mad but the seagulls weren't just flying, they were following something going against the tide, and what they were following was moving under the surface along the winding deep water channel that the big ships use, you know the way it twists and turns... if it didn't they wouldn't need the pilot,' he finished defensively.

'Mmm,' said Geraldine, 'I thought we'd proved - to your satisfaction at least - that the birds followed the key when it was actually touching someone, as if that action activated whatever it is you believe transmits to the birds. Surely they wouldn't be interested in the person without the key, and the person had put the key under the boat. Poor Adam was being swept away in the opposite direction to the birds. It doesn't make sense to say they were still following him. He couldn't possibly be going against the tide underwater. It's mad.'

'I don't know,' said James, 'I can't explain it, perhaps Adam was different, perhaps they were after him as well as the key. If they were honed in on him they wouldn't necessarily know he had left the key somewhere.'

'Like when I perform a brilliant dummy on the football field and the opponents don't realise it until I score a goal,' said Mugsy.

James smiled, 'something like that Mugsy, but the birds must know by now they've been sold a dummy, that they may have Adam but not the key. I don't know but I just think he's still alive and that's why his body hasn't been found. On that day the birds were headed towards the Ness. Well, we were on the Ness today when we unwrapped the key and all of a sudden the birds appeared. It's all very strange, and the Ness is at the centre of it all.' Something struck him as he dredged a thought from the back of his mind.

'Of course! The boy didn't say the Watchers on the rock at all. He said the Watchers in the rocks.' He turned round and stared at the cliff face, 'whatever we're looking for, it's in the Ness, not on it.'

Chapter Five

'Well, well, if it isn't Professor Cheat!'

James looked round from the bakery window, where he was considering the merits of an Eccles cake versus a Chelsea bun.

'Alex, I didn't cheat, you crashed into me, you weren't looking where you were going, you were way off course and tried to get over as fast as possible when you realised. I don't think it was deliberate.'

'That's not how I remember it. I was all set to win and you couldn't stand the idea of someone beating you.'

'What did the umpire say? You went and complained to him.'

Alex blushed, then his face darkened. 'What does he know, the silly old fool? He's blind as a bat when it suits him. I'll get my dad to have him replaced. You'd just better keep out of my way on Wednesday.'

'Wednesday?'

'I assume you're going to compete in the Otter sailing race and you'll be hoping - and I use the word hoping - to win one of the cups in the rowing races in the afternoon.'

'Yes, I'll be there,' James admitted reluctantly.

'I'll see if I can get that fool of an umpire disqualified by then and get someone who can see more than six inches in front of their face.' Alex strode across the road past the newsagent and down Albion Street where he lived.

James sighed. His appetite had gone, it hadn't been a good day yesterday and today had not started well either. That morning he had gone down to breakfast and Digger and Drum were sitting on the balcony rail staring in at him through the patio doors. He had placed the key in its lead holder inside his socks drawer last night and when he got up had slipped it into his pocket. The lead was heavy and bulky in his shorts and he had taken it out, removed the lead, put it on his bookshelf and taken a clean handkerchief out of his drawer. Then he had wrapped the object in it, stuffed it in his pocket with the zip and did it up firmly.

He had not had a good night, tossing and turning as he tried to make sense of the events of the last few days. A dead stranger, a mysterious key that Mugsy still insisted was part of an outboard engine, gulls that as Geraldine said in her matter of fact way, might or might not have followed people when they did or didn't have the key, but more likely were just greedy birds that liked ready salted crisps. To cap it all he had concocted some fantastic story around the flash of white he had thought he had seen when the boy had been swept away. Had the birds followed the winding deep-water channel? Weren't they just tracking mackerel or pilchards, which by their very nature didn't swim in a straight line but would dart around? Had anything untoward really happened? Was it just a tragic accident that he was trying to explain away, to massage away that kernel of guilt he felt, that he hadn't done anything to stop the boy when he had raced into the sea and drowned? Surely the movement of the seagulls were just coincidental and not really worthy of comment?

When the seagulls stared straight in at him as he ate breakfast he had fingered the key in his pocket. It was warm. The surface felt rubbery, it was a strange item, whatever its true provenance. He didn't believe it could be off an engine or anything remotely as prosaic as a barbecue handle.

As the final straw, Geraldine had lost in the finals of the rounders yesterday, to a team that included Alex's younger sister, Anna. Alex himself, who previously had shown no interest in what most boys of his age considered to be a girl's game, had seemed overly triumphant.

James looked at Einstein, stroked her head and said bitterly 'it's only rounders, it's not as if it's anything important like the cricket.' Then to cap it all Einstein had hurt herself when hurling her body at the patio doors in a frantic attempt to get at the seagulls. Einstein had always had a thing about gulls and these two seemed to goad her beyond endurance. The dog had gone to lie down in her basket after the collision and was very quiet, not even sitting next to him at breakfast, begging for a morsel.

Standing outside the bakers now, balancing an oar in each hand, James looked at Alex's disappearing back. He was sure to win in one of the swimming races that morning and was hot favourite, together with his family - who all seemed unnaturally sporty - to win the beach volleyball in the afternoon.

James was going down to watch Geraldine in the "girls over 12 but not yet 15" swimming contest. Alex was competing in the preceding race so if James wanted to watch her he would have to endure Alex's triumphalism if and when he won. Immediately after James was going for a row with Mugsy. Hopefully Geraldine would come and talk her blunt common sense that would make him realise that it was time to drop his silly obsession with the seagulls. He realised that he had to come to terms that the boy had died in a tragic accident and –here he blushed at the knowledge he had said such a thing aloud rather than kept it in his head – apologise for his comment that the Watchers were somehow inside the rock rather than on it. No-one else believed they existed at all, in, on, or under the Ness. He swung the oars determined to put it all behind him and just enjoy regatta week.

James couldn't decide whether to watch the volleyball, he wasn't really very keen on the game. Mugsy came along the road from the direction of Ringmore whistling tunelessly.

'Hi, Professor, why the long face? You look as if you've lost an oar and found a seagull, sorry, that wasn't very funny, was it?'

'Are they there?'

'Who? Oh, Digger and Drum. No there's no sign of... oh, yes, is that them on the roof of the Clifford Arms?' James swivelled round and looked at the roof of the pub just over the road.

'Yes, that looks like them, they either seem to continually follow me or failing that spend their time watching me all the time as if they're spying. No, that's fanciful. They've not tried to harass me at all, not like poor Adam.'

Mugsy nodded. 'He was trying to escape from them; perhaps they'd just taken a dislike to him and decided to make his life a misery. They wouldn't dare do that to you, Einstein would tear them limb from limb.'

'Yeah, she hates all seagulls and those two in particular; she nearly smashed through the patio doors this morning trying to get at them. I hope she's OK. She seemed a bit stunned after her collision.'

Mugsy murmured sympathetically then said, 'Did you get any cakes?'

'No, I didn't feel like it, anyway, shall we wander on down to the beach?'

'It's a bit early, isn't it?' Mugsy glanced at his watch. 'I'll just nip inside the bakers and get a doughnut to keep me going,' he reappeared a minute later clutching a bag. 'I got two just in case.'

'In case what?'

'In case I needed two. What's the time now?'

'One minute later than when you said it was too early,' replied James.

Mugsy opened the bag and started eating, holding the paper underneath to catch the jam that dripped out. 'Shall we go to the foreshore and see if there are any salmon leaping, then we can wander down to the main beach?'

'Ok, why not?'

They headed down Albion Street past the newsagent's. Mugsy finished the doughnut, licked his fingers and stuffed the spare in his pocket. 'I know, let's go via the village green, I lost a pound coin there last week, it might be worth looking for it.'

'You're hopeful,' said James.

'Perhaps someone has taken my £1 coin and dropped a £2 one, you've got to look on the bright side.' They walked past the giant eucalyptus tree and turned right, past the bowls green, which as usual was populated by older people intent on a match. Then they passed Potters Mooring Hotel and the London inn and turned right on to the village green which was lined with flower planters full of Busy Lizzies and Petunias.

'Wow! Look at the state of it,' exclaimed Mugsy, 'looks as if its been baked in an oven! I've never seen the grass look so brown.'

'It has a lot of use at this time of the year,' said James, 'the carnival, dances, church meetings, fetes, the 1785 Day and now the regatta. And there hasn't been any rain for weeks.'

'I was going to be in that, but I had too much homework so I didn't have the time.'

'I'm lost,' said James, 'you are in the regatta. Or are you a mirage?'

'No, not that, the 1785 day.'

James looked askance at his friend. 'The 1785 Day? 'Isn't that when some of the villagers dress up in old-fashioned costumes and try to flog crafts to visitors? I've only been once, really boring, who wants to buy quilts or cushions or pictures and things?'

'Adults,' said Mugsy meaningfully. 'You know what they're like.'

1785 Day was held on summer Wednesdays, reflecting Shaldon's history that was closely linked to a period around the end of the 18th century. The bunting, the stalls, the dressing up in period costume by villagers presiding over craft stalls, was considered an integral part of Shaldon's charm by visitors, but viewed with complete incomprehension by most of the younger population.

'No, I wasn't going to sell crafts or anything. I was going to be in one of the crowd scenes for the evening entertainment.'

James almost choked with laughter, 'you were going to be in the Punch and Judy show? What, dressing up as the crocodile?'

Mugsy waited patiently for James to finish chortling. 'No, that alternates with the play, the one with Zebediah Hook the Shaldon Smuggler, there was to be a battle or something, anyway I didn't after all. I wish I had taken part though because it was supposed to be really good.'

'Smuggling,' said James thoughtfully, 'smuggling... Ness cove...the smugglers' tunnel, perhaps that's it, high-tech smugglers!'

'You're not going to recite the smugglers song again, are you?' asked Mugsy anxiously 'I really couldn't bear it. Anyway, what are you thinking they might be smuggling, assuming that anything strange is going on which remains to be proved. Drugs? Cigarettes? People?'

'I don't know, but that could be it, the docks are just opposite Ness cove but it can't be seen at all. Stuff could be brought in by the big ships, hidden in their holds under everyone's nose and then popped into a speedboat and shipped over to Ness Cove. Or shipped over using a submarine.'

'Don't start that again,' said Mugsy, 'a speedboat might be possible, but where is the point in taking stuff to Ness Cove, it would then have to be hauled right up all those flights of steps. If I were smuggling I'd take it by boat to... say, the cove by the Carey Arms at

Babbacombe, that's next to the road, although it's a bit public. Or even better, I'd go right up the river to Newton Abbot and unload at the old wharf, no one ever goes there, that'd be a great place, no one would think of even putting the words "Newton Abbot" and "smugglers" into the same sentence.'

'But if they went to the Ness,' said James, 'it would all fit, they wouldn't need to lug it up the stairs would they if they were to actually go inside the Ness?'

'Hmm,' said Mugsy, 'you'd better not say anything about this to Alex or he'll think that you're a drizzoid. Ah, what's this?' he continued, bending low to the ground, 'and speaking of fitting, this will fit nicely into my pocket.' With that he picked up a £2 coin.

'You lucky devil!' exclaimed James, 'looks like the ice creams are on you then!'

'I fancy a bar of chocolate not an ice cream,' said Mugsy thoughtfully, 'one of those really big bars. Let's go to the Spar, they sell them there.'

***

Alex had won his swimming race by a mile and Geraldine had also duly won hers. When the photographs were taken for the local paper Alex had tried to put his arm round her shoulders and Geraldine had angrily shrugged it off.

'Who does he think he is?' she said to no one in particular once the photos were completed.

'Nice, very nice,' Alex called over appreciatively. Bas laughed. Geraldine slipped a towelling robe over her swimsuit.

'Hi James, thanks for coming,' she planted a kiss on his cheek and as James turned towards him he could see Alex's face was as dark as thunder. Bas grasped him by the shoulder and the pair walked off.

'What's happening this morning? Have you made any plans? I'm meeting my parents on the beach at one o' clock for lunch, and then we're staying for the volleyball. We've got an hour, did you want to try and dig your way into the middle of the Ness to find your Watchers?'

'Don't tease. I think I might have found a reason for all these strange goings-on.'

'An over-active imagination?' rejoindered Geraldine.

'Ouch, that hurts,' said James ruefully.

'Sorry, I'm listening.'

'Smugglers.'

Her eyes opened wide. 'Here in Shaldon? I know it used to go on but that was in the olden days before even my parents were born.'

'Anyway, we were thinking of going for a row.'

'Oh, so that's why you're carrying oars, I thought you were going to dig your parents' allotment.'

'Very funny... you're in a skittish mood today, listen, I thought we could have a row over by the docks and see if there is anything suspicious going on.'

'Did you?' said Mugsy, 'you hadn't said anything to me, what do you expect to find?'

'I don't know,' said James vaguely, 'we might be able to see suspicious goods being unloaded, or things hidden under tarpaulins or there might be strange characters wandering about.'

'There's always strange characters wandering about,' said Mugsy, 'they're called visitors.'

'Anyway,' concluded James, 'it can't do any harm and it will give us some good practice, especially if Geraldine can come along as extra ballast.'

'Thank you very much, that's how you see me, is it? Not as a beautiful, clever, modest and intelligent girl, but as ballast.'

'Oh, crumbs!' said James, ' No, no, what I meant was that it will be good practice to have the extra weight in the boat.'

'So I'm heavy now, am I? You look on me as a replacement for sand bags or something?' She burst into a big laugh and James sighed.

'You're teasing me again, let's just go, shall we?'

'Help me into the boat, will you, James?' she held his hand for support as she clambered into the boat, holding it a little longer than seemed necessary.

James said, 'I don't know what you're smirking at Mugsy.'

The tide was full in so they were able to row straight across the Salty, directly to the docks. At low tide the Salty rises like a giant shell encrusted island out of the water and at that state of the tide becomes a popular area for paddling. Beyond it, the river flows at all states of the tide to within a hundred yards of the docks.

They rowed towards Gales Hill, where fishermen repair lobster pots and lay out nets and other paraphernalia, and where the towns' remnants of a fishing fleet would sometimes moor. In order to get more exercise they turned the Lucy Ann so they could row past the beach huts on the Point, crowded with people enjoying picnics, preparing for fishing trips, boat rides to Brixham, or waiting for the little black and white ferry to transport them over to Shaldon.

Then they turned again at the estuary mouth and followed the course of the river, picking their way through the numerous boats, which reappeared from hibernation in the summer, moored to their single buoys. The beginning of the docks was marked by a large blue warehouse that stood back some twenty yards from the edge of the quay on which it sat. A huge ship - the Maid of Holland - was tied up. There was a lot of activity with lorries going backwards and forwards emitting their high-pitched warning signals as they reversed.

'You should have been here a few weeks ago Geraldine,' remarked James as they rowed slowly past, scanning the cargo. 'There was a theatre ship moored for a few days, it was going round the coast performing 20,000 Leagues Under the Sea. It was really good, I went with my parents and Mugsy.'

'Yes, it was good,' admitted Mugsy reluctantly, 'but then again they didn't have any poetry in it.' He stopped rowing for a second and the boat drifted slowly as the current gently spun it round. 'What exactly are we looking for? Gold bars, barrels of brandy? Would you like to tell me - without reciting that poem again,' he said firmly as Geraldine started:

'Face the wall my darling... I like poetry,' she said simply, 'especially the romantic stuff, we learnt a lot of Byron last term.' James and Mugsy groaned in unison and restarted rowing.

'We're looking for nothing too obvious,' said James, 'they're hardly likely to have gold bars stacked up on the quayside or large wooden boxes marked "contraband" being moved by fork lift trucks.'

'Mind that yacht,' warned Geraldine who was sitting in the stern watching the way ahead. A large white yacht was swinging round to tie up at one of the visitor's moorings.

'There are a lot of boats out and about,' said Mugsy, 'look at all the dinghies moored up to the swinging moorings.'

'It would be very easy to smuggle stuff,' conceded Geraldine reluctantly, 'the ships moor just over there and it would be simple to bring a small boat alongside them in the dead of night, you'd only see that happening from the Shaldon side, and if it was at low tide the Salty would hide a lot of the view anyway. You wouldn't really see much from the Teignmouth side as those large blue warehouses screen the view. Wood!' she said suddenly, 'perhaps they're smuggling wood. If they are it's the most brazen smuggling ever, there are heaps of it on the quay, great big long planks.'

'There's not much money in wood surely,' said James doubtfully.

'I don't know about that,' said Mugsy, 'my dad buys wood sometimes and he says the people selling it must be pirates. That's almost the same as smugglers.'

'Still,' protested James, who had half stopped rowing, causing the boat to swing almost completely round in the current, enabling him to get a better view, 'it would have to be on a vast scale, wood is very heavy and bulky. You're not going to make a fortune just smuggling one piece are you, and it's not very easy to hide either, wood is one of the most noticeable things there is.'

'Don't you think it's sometimes better to be brazen?' said Geraldine, 'you're much more likely to get away with it if you're bold, rather than shuffling along not looking anyone in the eye.'

'That may be so,' agreed James, 'but it still doesn't get away from the fact you'd have to do it on a vast scale, and wood is not the most easily handled or lightest of materials, you wouldn't be able to hide much in the bilges of a speed boat for example, not like cigarettes or drugs.'

'Perhaps you're right,' nodded Geraldine, 'look at those two men on the quay there, they can barely lift that plank, the one that's gone skewiff on the pile.'

'Hmm,' said Mugsy unconvinced, 'perhaps they haven't had their spinach yet today, look, that other man has straightened up that other pile with one hand,' he pointed and James looked over.

'Keep your head down,' he said suddenly, 'don't let him see you, row slowly towards the quay so we can get a better look.'

'If we go in too much closer,' protested Mugsy, 'we'll be inside the ship's hold. I can practically clean the side of this boat. What is it?'

'That person doing the lifting, it's the boy.'

'What! But he drowned, we saw him, it can't be.'

'I'll swivel round a bit so you can see, don't point or anything. What do you think?'

'Hmm,' said Mugsy, 'I only caught a brief look at Adam, but whilst his build and features are very similar, that person just over there is much larger. He's an adult, not a child.'

Geraldine whispered, 'Swing round a bit more, James, so I can… there, that's it, I've got a good view. I'd say that's a full grown man, you said the person who drowned was a boy about your age and a bit smaller than you.'

The man had gone to the edge of the quay and seemed to be fiddling with something on the quay wall. Then he saw them looking, turned smartly on his heel and walked into the warehouse.

'They're very similar in appearance,' agreed Mugsy, 'perhaps it's his father.'

'No one came forward,' countered James, 'they were saying that on the local news this morning. Everyone round here knows what happened, if his father worked at the docks he couldn't fail to have heard.'

'It was obviously someone just like the boy but rather bigger,' said Geraldine diplomatically. 'They're called doppelgangers aren't they?'

'Doppel who?' asked Mugsy.

'Gangers, it means two different people who are virtually identical to each other; it causes all sorts of confusion. It was just a coincidence; come on, we need to get going; it's getting on for one o'clock. I'm inclined to agree with Mugsy that timber would be good for smuggling, I had been half joking when I said about it, but the more I think of the rewards...' she continued, as Mugsy and James struck off towards the Shaldon river beach. They rowed straight over the Salty again, its mussels magnified by the clear water that wavered as the tide flowed steadily out.

'Hardwood from tropical rain forests would be very valuable, we did a project on it,' said Geraldine suddenly.

'Everyone does projects on rainforests,' sighed Mugsy, 'I think it's obligatory for schools, or perhaps they can't think of anything else to occupy us with.'

'It has great density…' continued Geraldine.

'We know,' said Mugsy desperately.

'So that makes it very heavy, even a small piece would be…'

Mugsy deliberately hit the water hard with his oar splashing her.

'So I take it you're not interested in hearing my learned thoughts on rainforests and their sustainability? Still, it's your loss. Anyway, are you two coming to watch me play volleyball this afternoon? The Surrey Superstars are trained to a peak of physical perfection. We are going to be awesome.'

'So is Alex and his family,' said Mugsy gloomily, 'the Shaldon Strollers they're calling themselves. His dad is some bigwig in the army, isn't he? Probably does lots of training and is sickeningly fit.'

'Just drop me by the ferry point if you would,' said Geraldine, 'my family said they'd bag a place on the beach. My word, it's crowded! It looks like one of those documentaries when the beach is covered in penguins and no one can move without stepping on someone else's eggs.'

James had been deep in thought and came out of his reverie to hear the last bit of this conversation.

'What penguins?' he asked, 'we have seals in the harbour sometimes, but I've never seen penguins. Anyway Gerry, there are your parents, they're sitting by Lucy Ann's place on the beach. At least I won't have to turf any visitors off, they don't like it when I tell them they're in the way.'

***

James walked into his garden. He had agreed to go down at 3pm to see the finals and semi finals, but had excused himself from the volleyball preliminaries, as he wanted to see how Einstein was faring, following her encounter with the patio doors that morning.

'That daft dog just doesn't seem to understand the concept of glass, if the path ahead looks clear she thinks she must be able to walk through it,' he had said to Geraldine's father, Stephen Robertson, who had helped him to haul Lucy Ann up the beach on condition they could use the hull as a table. 'Even if he had bumped into it a second before, he would still try to walk through it again a second later.' As James left he almost tripped over the Duck Man who gave him a frightful glare.

'What have you done to upset him?' said Mr Robertson, 'and what happened to the old one? He was nice.'

'It wouldn't surprise me if he's been murdered,' said James, 'this new Duck Man is pretty odd. And I don't know what I'm supposed to have done to him either,' he pointed towards Alex who was standing talking to Bas and Ritchie.

'He makes no friend who never made a foe, isn't that how the poem goes?'

James considered that for a moment, 'perhaps it's true, who said it?'

'Alfred Lord Tennyson, if you've got to make enemies in order to have friends, perhaps it's a reasonable trade off in life.'

James opened the door to his house and was immediately submerged by Einstein who jumped up at him barking furiously. James walked through into the kitchen to get her a biscuit from the cupboard. Mum was making lunch.

'Hello mum. Einstein is OK then, I see.'

'Oh, yes, about half an hour after you went out she got up from her basket, went to her dog bowl for a drink then barked madly at someone who had the effrontery to put a leaflet through the front door. I think she might have been a bit concussed straight after her accident, that's why she went quiet for a little while.'

'What was the leaflet about?'

'I don't know, she completely shredded it, postmen and seagulls, those are her prime hates at the moment, anyway, as you can see she's fully recovered.'

After they had all finished lunch Mum said;

'Dad and I are strolling down to the beach to watch the start of the volleyball. Geraldine is in it isn't she? We don't really want to take Einstein, she's not allowed on the beach anyway and isn't very good in crowds.'

'Ok, I'll stay here until just before three,' said James, 'I promised Geraldine I'd come and watch her triumph if she managed to get as far as the semi finals.'

'We might see you down there then,' said mum, 'don't forget to lock up and make sure you shut the windows, we don't want anyone to complain about her barking if someone comes to the door, you know how that sets her off.'

His parents had gone. James got a piece of paper from the computer printer and a pen from the kitchen drawer. Then he opened wide the patio door leading onto the balcony. He wanted to get all that had happened clear in his own mind and then write down the key points in sequence, to try and work out what was happening - if anything. That figure on the dock was just the latest in a long list of strange things but as Gerry had said, people did have doppelgangers. He touched the key in his pocket which had been hidden in his sock drawer whilst he was out and that he had just recovered, taking off the lead cover so he could examine it properly.

As he looked Digger and Drum flew onto the fence that separated his house from their neighbours. Einstein growled loudly from her vantage point on the sofa. James turned round to look at her then glanced back at the birds, and then before he knew what was happening Digger flew towards him, scratched his face, grabbed the pen from his hand and then retired to the balcony rail just a few feet away to gaze at him. It screeched loudly twice, pen held tightly in its claws.

Goaded beyond endurance Einstein ran forward and leapt at the bird. Whether Digger or Einstein were more surprised at the lack of glass separating them no one can say, but the dog's leap carried her onto Digger, who slammed against the balcony balustrade, and then the pair of them went crashing over the rail and fell onto the patio below.

'Einstein!' James stood up, horrified and rushed to look over the balcony, fearful of what he might see. The dog was already on her feet and was worrying the bird that she had clenched firmly between her teeth, shaking it this way and that. James rushed to the stairs and clattered down onto the patio.

'Ok Einstein, good dog, put it down... down.' He grabbed the dog's collar and with difficulty forced her to drop the gull and pulled her inside the house. 'Sit... sit.' He looked her over carefully for grazes and lifted each paw gently in turn to make sure there were no cuts on them. Einstein continued to growl, and every now and then let out a defiant bark.

'Good girl, brave dog, here, let's get a biscuit for you.' He got one from the kitchen cupboard and left Einstein eating it on the hall floor. Then he walked through to the balcony, Drum was looking very hard at him. Digger was still lying inert on the patio where it had been left.

James grabbed his coat from the peg, ran down the stairs and threw it over the bird, thinking that any moment it would recover and attack him again. Then he opened the door to his workshop at the back of the garage under the house, went inside and shut it firmly. He carried the bird carefully to the bench, which was littered with pieces of metal, cable, wood and bits of computer that were used in increasingly ambitious experiments, and attempts to create gadgets of varying complexity and scientific worth.

He found a space and laid the seagull carefully on it. There was a loud thump against the door, then another and he heard a terrible squawking. James looked up startled, 'What's that? It must be Drum, still, he can't break through a solid wooden door can he?' The banging redoubled and the door shook.

James returned to the bird and removed the coat. The gull seemed in perfect condition, there was no sign of blood or any wound. Still convinced the creature was merely concussed, James slipped on a pair of Dad's gardening gloves in order to hold the bird firmly and provide protection from the curved beak, should the gull recover.

The banging against the door continued and was then replaced by a steady rhythmic tapping. James looked up alarmed, 'he's trying to peck a way through...' a piece of wood splintered from the door, then another. Then there was a furious series of taps and a piece of wood several inches square flew off on to the floor and a sharp, evil-looking beak appeared. Then the tapping stopped and a second later the door swung open;

'James, are you in there?' asked dad, 'that seagull seemed to be attacking the door. I had to throw a stone at it, the wretched thing didn't seem to want to go - are you OK?'

'I'm fine, dad,' said James, throwing the coat over Digger to hide the inert figure. 'So that's what the banging was,' he tried to keep his voice steady and regain composure. Badly shaken, his heart was still racing.

'I'll go and call the council,' said Dad, 'these seagulls are getting very aggressive, the trouble is the visitors will feed them, despite all the signs up asking them not to. They will give them chips and pieces of sandwich. It just makes the wretched birds bolder and bolder, sure you're OK? The creature was demented. Perhaps it's got some sort of disease.'

'I'm fine dad.'

His father went out and James sat down heavily on the chair, his legs suddenly weak. He felt faint and a bit sick and had to sit still for a minute breathing heavily.

Then he bent over the inert figure, removed the coat and looked more closely at the bird, no longer afraid it would suddenly come back to life. There were still no traces of blood. He turned it over gingerly on to its back.

'I wonder why it suddenly decided to attack me? Of

course! I was holding that very chunky silver pen - it looks rather like the key. It was trying to grab it from me,' he got onto his knees and stared hard at the gull, there was a strange circular mark on its neck, almost hidden under its neck feathers.

He touched it curiously and the bird made a slight hum. Startled, James moved his finger. The hum immediately stopped. Hesitating for a moment he picked the creature up then settled himself firmly in his chair, stretched out his finger and touched the mark again. The hum restarted, then a line appeared vertically down the birds breastbone as the bird split in two, revealing a maze of strange wiring and blobs of a metal and plastics he did not recognise. James breathed out sharply.

'It's just like Adam said - it's a mechanical!'

Chapter Six

THE phone rang then mum called up the stairs, 'James, it's Geraldine.'

'Geraldine?' He sat up in bed staring blankly at the gap in the curtain that the sun was shining through.

He turned over and picked up the watch from the bedside chest of drawers

'James are you coming?'

'Would you ask her to hold on a minute?' he looked at the watch, 8.30, why would…oh no, he groaned, he'd said that he would go to see her and her family in the volleyball yesterday afternoon, but in all the excitement had totally forgotten and had not phoned to explain…

'Crumbs, she'll be hopping mad,' he murmured uneasily, as he got out of bed, put on his dressing gown and walked slowly downstairs.

Mum held out the phone to him, 'It's Geraldine, and she doesn't sound a happy bunny.'

James grasped the phone, walked into the dining room then took a deep breath before putting the phone to his ear. 'Gerry, how are you?' he said cheerfully.

'Oh, so you remember who I am now do you? Where were you yesterday?'

'Look, I'm so sorry but…'

'It's a two way thing James, I come and support you and you come and support me, or do you think the things you do are more important than the ones I'm involved in?'

'Finished?'

'Yes, for the minute, but I'm winding myself up to have another go at you in a minute so don't relax just yet.'

'Well if you'd listen for just a moment...' he unlocked the French doors and walked out to sit on the patio, as far away as he could get from his parents, not wanting them to overhear their conversation.

'Look I'm sorry, but I was attacked yesterday afternoon.'

'Attacked?' Gerry's tone changed immediately. 'What do you mean? Who did it, it wasn't Alex, was it? I know he's pretty mad with you but I can't believe he'd do anything like that.'

'Gerry, will you just listen?' James smiled to himself, she always managed to raise his spirits even when he couldn't get a word in edgeways. 'It was the seagulls.'

'Seagulls?' There was a long pause. 'A seagull attacked you so badly you were unable to hobble down to the beach to see me?'

'Yes... no...' the sun was shining full into his face so he turned the chair round, 'yes Digger, one of the two seagulls, attacked me. I think it must have been after the key, I was holding a large silver pen that must have looked very similar. Einstein went completely berserk and attacked the thing. I thought she'd killed it.'

'Was it dead or did it get up and fly away?'

'No, she managed to get hold of it in her mouth when she rushed out from the balcony, I think she was as surprised as the seagull when it was actually caught, they must have both thought there would be glass in the way.'

'I'm not sure Einstein fully understands the concept of glass but never mind.'

'Anyway, her momentum carried her over the balcony rail with the seagull in her mouth and then she fell on top of it on to the patio.'

'She jumped over the balcony, is she OK?'

'Yes, fine, she just shook her head, worried the seagull a bit and then I took her inside to make sure there was no harm done.'

'What about the seagull?'

'Well, I rushed down and picked it up.'

'Uurgh!' said Geraldine, 'Was it all chewed bones and blood?'

'No, that was the strange thing, it was completely unmarked. Well the other seagull just stared at me, it didn't seem to know what to do, so I took Digger into my workshop and shut the door.'

'What did your parents say, had they seen what happened?'

'No, they'd come down to see you.'

'I'm glad someone from the Smith household did.'

James smiled again, Gerry did like to know all the details; she was a bit like that, rather similar to him, meticulous in getting to know all the facts then plan accordingly. Mugsy was quite the opposite; he was just spontaneous and never seemed to think ahead.

'James, are you still there?'

'Sorry, I was just thinking; well, I put Digger down on the floor and Drum started attacking the door - and I mean really attacking it, he took great chunks off.'

'Really? I didn't know seagulls were that strong, although when you see them tearing mussels off rocks you can see their power, especially in the beak. Perhaps this seagull is a tourist. The local ones don't tend to tear... they've all gone soft through the visitors feeding them chips and sandwiches and crisps.'

James laughed, 'I hadn't thought of that - seagulls here on holiday! It's a nice idea; anyway, it became seriously angry and thudded against the garage door, really shaking it. I thought it was going to come off its hinges and you know how strong these doors are, solid wood. Then it took a big chunk out and sort of stared in.'

'Oh, James, that's awful, but perhaps it was just trying to rescue its mate, don't they pair for life, or is that swans? Love can do strange things, you know.'

'You've been reading too many of your romantic poems. Well, dad came back at that moment and Drum must have flown off, but the point is - if you'll ever let me get that far - is that when I examined Digger...'

'You examined it, are you hoping to be a vet or something? That's a bit gruesome.'

James laughed, 'what's your email address?'

'Email?'

'Yes, I can write to let you know what happened as you won't let me tell you, then you can read about it at your convenience.'

'Ooops, sorry!'

'Well, I looked closely all over the thing as it seemed so strange that there was no sign of blood or any damage... pretty remarkable as a mad dog had squashed it then chewed it. I sort of pressed something on its neck and it opened.'

'What do you mean opened? Uurrggh! You mean it spilt out its guts like fish do when they're filleted?'

'No, it was more like a DVD drawer opening, soft and smooth and a slight hum and a click. It's a mechanical, Gerry, or electronic, more like, it's stuffed full off all sorts of bits and pieces like you'd find if you took a computer apart, but not in a style or material that I've ever come across.'

There was a silence.

'Gerry are you there?'

'Yes, you just gave me a bit of shock, well a lot of a shock actually.'

James shifted in his seat.

'Listen, I need to get ready for the Otter dinghy sailing, it starts at 10, I'm in the first race with my dad, I'm going to helm.'

'Yes, my dad is in it as well.'

'What age group is he in?'

'He wouldn't say, but he'll have to come clean when he puts his entry form in, so when the races start I'll know.'

'Anyway, despite me being a beast for not coming to support you yesterday, will you be down in time for the first race? Mugsy is coming to cheer me on, but you know him, he prefers oars to sails, so he's not actually competing in anything.'

'Of course I will.'

'Then I thought we could have a chat about it. The mechanical that is. I've no idea what it all means. I need to talk it through.'

'Have you finished for the day after the sailing?'

'No, it's rowing all afternoon with the Regatta dinghies, then it's the Seine boat racing at 5.30, my mums rowing in that, in the "Old Bats" trophy.'

'Old bats! That's a bit rude, isn't it?'

'It's the veterans trophy for women over 45, you have to have a good sense of humour to live in Shaldon, you know.'

'Ok, I'll see you at 10. Haven't you forgotten something?'

'What's that?'

You haven't asked me how we got on.'

'I already know, you were knocked out in the first heat so even if I had come down at three o'clock yesterday afternoon I wouldn't have seen you competing, would I?'

'How did you know? Of course! Your parents were there, and you were letting me rant on when you knew all the time... see you later - and James... be careful.'

The phone went dead and James walked slowly inside and put the receiver back on its charging cradle in the hall.

'Would you like a fried breakfast?' asked mum as he came into the kitchen, 'me and dad are going to have one to get our strength up for later, what with me being a poor weak old bat and your dad having to admit he's a veteran. He's racing in a crew with Geraldine's dad and... is it her uncle? The one that has that smart boat... the one with the huge engine that looks as if it fell off a jumbo jet. Did she mention it?'

'Sort of.'

Mum went to the patio doors to open them in preparation for breakfast on the balcony.

'Gosh, smell that salt, funny how sometimes you get a great whiff of it all of a sudden'

'The wind's getting up a bit and the tide's coming in, so the waters getting agitated,' said dad looking up from his paper.

'Speaking of agitation and salt,' remarked mum.

'Oh, no!' said James, who knew what was coming.

'Yes, you said you'd make a start on that holiday project you've got to do for school, the one about salt.'

'There's plenty of time, and it's such a deadly dull subject, there ought to be a law against it.'

'We had to suffer at school,' said dad unsympathetically, 'so I don't see why you shouldn't as well, it's natural justice, anyway it's a jolly interesting subject. It lost the British their empire in India when Gandhi decided to trudge thousands of miles to the sea and make his own salt.'

'Couldn't he buy it in a shop?'

'You have a lot to learn,' said dad sighing, 'all they seem to teach about history these days is how to empathise with Mary Queen of Scots before she had her head cut off, or more likely with some peasant who never did anything more exciting than get scurvy.'

'Dad!' said James, 'you can't say that sort of thing; anyway, I'll get on with it of course, but not until the regattas over. There will still be masses of time before the holiday ends.'

A piece of toast popped up and they went back in the kitchen and mum broke an egg in the frying pan. 'You'll be back for lunch won't you, after you finish your epic sailing race with dad? Now you've got about 30 seconds to get dressed while this egg cooks, and Einstein is waiting here with mouth open, obviously banking on you not making it back in that time.'

***

'We were going into Torquay this evening to celebrate our wins at the races this afternoon, we're going to call it the batty old veterans evening, Geraldine's mum and dad and her uncle and his wife are coming. Geraldine said she would come if you did.'

James had been sitting at his workbench trying to follow the circuitry of the seagull when the garage door had opened, and quickly placed an old blanket he had brought down for the purpose, over the remains of Digger.

'Yes mum, great, although I'm not sure a second place for me is worth celebrating.'

'That's why we're dedicating it to batty old veterans, you've got plenty of chances to win. Us bats on the other hand are coming to the twilight of their brilliant careers.'

James smiled, 'it wouldn't have mattered so much if I hadn't been beaten by Alex of all people.'

'You were unlucky,' said mum, 'the wind dropped just as you were doing that tack, it happens to all of us.'

'Where are you going?'

'Pizza Express on Torquay harbour, we want to see that swish new pedestrian bridge everyone's talking about. The one near the "Living Coasts." We want to have a shower first and a bit of a sit down, our race was only an hour or so ago so we need to rest our aching and ancient bones. We'll probably leave in about three quarters of an hour, about eight o clock or so. Hopefully when we finish the pizza the lights around the harbour will be on, the nights are starting to draw in now of course. End of August already, it doesn't see possible. The shops will have their Christmas stuff in before we know it'

James looked at his watch 'Ok, I'll come up and get ready in half an hour or so.'

Mum withdrew from the workshop and shut the door. When he was sure she was gone James unwrapped the mechanical again.

He had managed to disconnect five of the internal parts and believed he had identified their purpose. He picked one up and looked at it carefully, still not recognising the material nor the nature of the construction, there were no screws or solder or anything that looked like a computer chip. However, it all seemed to slot together in a highly intuitive way. The piece in his hand was probably a camera, although he hadn't seen one that tiny, even in a James Bond film.

The next piece seemed to be some sort of transmitter, rather like the radio control used in conjunction with the model airplane he had bought a couple of years previously. That had met with an unfortunate accident after colliding with a tree on top of the Haldon Hills. An appropriate place to fly an airplane he had thought, as it had used to be an aerodrome. James had taken the remains home and completely dismantled both the plane and the transmitter in order to better understand how they worked. He glanced up at the neatly labelled boxes on the shelves above the bench; somehow there had never been the time to reassemble it.

The transmitter would presumably give instructions to the bird. It would be tracked on a screen so the operator could see what was happening via the camera that would direct the bird's movements accordingly. He picked up the camera again and examined it closely; if only there was some sort of a screen to watch he could perhaps reassemble the bird and try to fly it. At the least, even without a screen it would be interesting to try, though whether he would be able to see what was happening in order to guide the mechanical properly he didn't know. The trouble was the bird was completely inactive; there was no sign of movement in any of the parts. Presumably some thing must have been knocked loose within the sealed body that couldn't be accessed. That would probably have happened when Einstein had attacked it. Or perhaps the operators in the Ness had turned the power off when the bird had disappeared from their screens. He smiled to himself. He wondered what the other two would think of his theory that there were people hidden within the Ness operating a mechanical seagull!

'But it isn't completely dead, is it?' murmured James to Einstein, who was sitting at his feet hoping for some of the tuck kept in a tin on one of the shelves. He patted the dog's head and ruffled her fur. 'I pressed that concealed button and the bird opened up. Ah, of course! Presumably it's got some sort of fail-safe mechanism, it won't work until it has all been put back together correctly and resealed.'

James stared hard at the seagull. 'Surely something must have been damaged in the first place or it wouldn't have died like it did when Einstein attacked it...? unless...' he examined the mark on the neck that he had touched to open up the bird. He pressed it gently, then pressed it again.

'That must be it - it's some sort of two stage switch, to access it you need to touch it a second time when the power has been turned off. The power must have been accidentally turned off either when Einstein grabbed it round the neck or when it hit the floor. You've done something like that before, haven't you, girl, when you sometimes walk over the TV remote and turn on the television accidentally? At least I assume it's accidental. Perhaps you secretly watch tv when we're all out?'

He stroked the dog's head then looked at his watch, tempted to put everything together again and then see if somehow the key could be used as the transmitter.

James was sure the key had played a part in the gulls being such a nuisance, and if the birds could home in on it, it might be possible to use it to control them. He took the lead encased object from the shelf where it had been temporarily placed in a tin box and wiggled it in his hand. 'No, there's no time, it's going to take more than a couple of minutes to try and work out everything isn't it?' Einstein licked his hand in agreement. James carefully wrapped the bird and its components in the blanket; mum was coming in during the morning - probably before he got up - in order to give the place a clean. A weekly clean had been one of the provisos for being allowed to use this part of the garage. It led off from several other rooms, one of which dad used as an office and the other that Mum created her paintings in. Dad had firmly said he couldn't work surrounded by clutter, no matter how artistic it might be.

He took down the picture from the wall that Mum had painted of the Lucy Ann, and opened the hatch that was hidden behind, that led into the under-house. He pushed the blanket through with the figure safely encased within its folds, then almost as an afterthought placed the key in after it, replaced the hatch and picture and opened the garage doors.

Coming out he glanced over the fence, the Duck Man was next door. The man placed a small package outside the neighbour's door then walked away.

'What's the Duck Man doing up here?' James thought, looking after the disappearing figure He must be following me. But why?' Then he went inside the house and walked up the stairs to change.

***

'Isn't that Alex over there? He's just come in with Bas and a few of the others.' Geraldine pointed. Pizza Express was crowded and there was a queue at the door.

'Oh, no, where?' said James.

'There, at the back of the queue. Good job we got here ahead of the rush.'

'Oh, yes, just my luck, he's probably celebrating his win. Still there's lots of tables, let's hope he isn't given one next to us.'

The adults were involved in deep conversations in between eating their starters of dough balls.

Gerry whispered, 'Are we going to get a chance to resurrect poor Digger tomorrow? I like the idea of flying a seagull around and dive bombing visitors.'

'Poor Digger!' exclaimed James indignantly, 'he nearly took my finger off when he grabbed what he thought was the key, anyway you're a visitor as well.'

'Not really, I'm an honorary resident, the amount of holiday we spend down here.'

'It would be good to put him together again,' replied James thoughtfully, 'but I'm not sure what time we'll have tomorrow. I'll have to look at the regatta programme. I'm in the rowing, but that's not until the early afternoon. '

'And I'm in the water sports again, only one of them though; I'm not eligible for the rest. I'm too old, too young, or not local enough. That race starts at 12.30.'

'And we said that all three of us would go in the treasure hunt by boat, that starts at 6.30,' said James.

Geraldine murmured, 'Alex and the others are being seated now. They're right at the front of the restaurant overlooking the street. I don't think he's seen us.'

'Good, he'll only find some reason to come over and gloat about his win. Anyway, that will give us two or three hours then between the races, probably from around three o clock or so, we should all be free then. If we could get Digger put back together and if we can find out how to use the key as a transmitter, we could fly him over the Ness, and see if the other birds come out to play.'

'That's a lot of ifs,' said Geraldine, 'but even better, we could fly him inside the Ness if you're so convinced something is going on in there. If we could lure the other seagulls out, we could see where they came from and follow them back in.'

'That's brilliant!' said James.

'I know,' said Geraldine, 'it's yet another example of my cleverly structured thinking.'

'Hmm, perhaps' said James, 'Look, Alex has got up and gone to the door, but the rest of his party have remained seated.'

'They're up to something,' said Geraldine, 'look at Bas and the others, they're giggling like schoolboys.'

'Where's he going? He's only been here for two minutes... and they are schoolboys,' said James as an afterthought, then more indignantly, 'and most of us don't giggle. He's gone out of the door, I think, I can't see what he's up to from here.'

'Look out, James,' said mum, 'the pizzas have arrived, take your elbow off the table or there won't be room - for pizzas that is, not elbows. It's a good job we arrived just before the rush; otherwise they might not have allowed us to push these two tables together. Margaret,' she turned to Geraldine's mother, 'I think this pasta was yours, and Stephen, I think you were having the pepperoni pizza with the extra topping? Jimmy and Stella, you were having the four seasons pizza, weren't you?' She directed the waiter to Geraldine's Uncle and Aunt. 'So you two must be sharing the Margherita pizza with pineapple, mushroom and ham. I'm not sure that still makes it a Margherita though, does it? Still, do you want some salad with it, anyone?'

'I'll have some,' said James.'

'None for me, thank you,' said Geraldine, 'we're supposed to be pacing ourselves as we both want puddings.'

The adults returned to their conversation, eating bits of pizza and pasta in between snatches of gossip.

'Alex has just come back in, what's that he's holding?' asked Geraldine nudging James.

'I can't really see, I think it's some sort of package done up in white paper.'

'Whatever it is, they're all giggling fit to burst.'

'Oh, no!' said James, 'I've heard of this, they're food surfing.'

'Food surfing,' said Geraldine in bewilderment, 'what on earth is that?'

'It's where a group go in to a restaurant and order part of a meal, and then they each take it in turns to surf round another food shop and bring something else back in to eat at the restaurant table.'

'I think Alex has brought in some fish and chips.'

'He wasn't long, he must have got them from the fish and chip shop opposite.'

Alex looked round him and surreptitiously unwrapped the package and passed it round under the table. Bas took something and almost choked on it as he was laughing so much. Then Alex put the package on the table and left it there unopened for a few seconds whilst each in turn took some food. Then he snatched it up and hid it under the table again.

'That must be part of the rules,' said Geraldine, trying to look at the scene without arousing her parents' comment. 'They have to leave it on the table in full view for a certain period whilst everyone helps themselves. It's rather childish,' She ate the last piece of pizza. 'What happens if they get caught?'

'I don't know, I've heard it's a bit of a craze but I've never seen it. Trust Alex to do something so stupid. Oh well, it's nothing to do with us. I wish the adults would hurry up, I've been eyeing up that lemon meringue all evening.'

***

Following the meal everyone walked round the harbour and ceremonially strolled over the new bridge. The general consensus was that it was an attractive structure that did a good job of linking both parts of the harbour. Previously there had been a big gap where the boats went in and out. Below the bridge there was now a sill to keep the water in a state of at least perpetual half tide.

'You wouldn't want visitors to see messy stuff like mud,' said Mr Robertson, 'everything must be tidied up nice and neat. Having said that, a bridge is a perfectly sensible idea, it means you can walk right round the harbour instead of having to turn back halfway. You wonder why no one thought of it years ago. Still I suppose they needed it to link up the Living Coasts with the various car parks and walk ways. Perhaps we'll have time to go there before we go back to Surrey.'

***

As soon as they got back home mum sensed something was wrong.

'I'd left the dustbin there by the back door ready to put out for tomorrow's collection, it's been moved.'

'Could be the wind,' said James, 'it seemed to get up a bit whilst we were walking round the harbour.'

'The door's ajar,' said dad, 'did you lock it? I think you were last out.'

'Of course I did.'

'Perhaps the wind's blown it open,' said James, 'if someone had accidentally forgotten to lock it, sometimes it doesn't always catch on the latch as you close it.'

'I definitely locked it,' said mum. 'I do know how to lock doors.'

Dad went into the hall and switched on the light. 'Where's that dog gone?'

Einstein came creeping down the stairs and half rolled onto her back in the hallway, wagging her tail.

'She's been under the bed,' said mum who was standing in the doorway, 'if she doesn't know who is in the house she sometimes goes there and hides.'

Dad opened the door to the living room, 'I don't remember shutting this, we don't normally close it. Oh no, you're right!'

'What's happened? I can't see, you're standing in the way.'

'The cupboard drawers have been tipped all over the floor, someone's been in here, it's a complete mess,' said dad.

Mum came in and stood by the sofa. 'Oh my goodness! Is anything missing?'

Dad bent down and picked through the items on the floor, 'nothing obvious as far as I can see, the television is still here and so are the video and the DVD player, what about...? yes, the music centre is still here as well. I'll go upstairs and have a look. You two stay there, they might still be around somewhere.'

'If Einstein was up there you can be sure the burglars aren't,' said mum.

Dad came down a few minutes later. 'Everything's all over the place, all the drawers have been upended and someone has been through the wardrobes. I can't see that anything has been stolen, though.'

'What about down in the garages?' said mum.

'Hmm…, I'll go and look.'

'I'll put the kettle on and make a nice cup of tea.'

'I'll come with you, dad.'

Dad turned on the outside lights and they went down the steps to find the garage door slightly ajar. 'The keys still in the lock,' said dad, 'it's our spare key, someone found it in the hiding place,' he pushed open the door and switched on the light. 'Mum's paintings seem alright. My office door has been opened. I'll just turn the light on,' he went in and turned round slowly, 'they don't seem to have taken anything, my radio and dictation machine are still here and so is my phone and printer… oh! The calculator's gone… no… wait, it was in the drawer, that's all over the floor of course but I can see the calculator. Look, the five pound note I put out as payment for your washing the car and doing that gardening is still there on the desk. That's strange, if a burglar doesn't even steal money what on earth can he be looking for? Oh, James!'

'What's up, dad?'

'Your room is in a state, I'm afraid, everything is on the floor, and your table's been turned over. What they were looking for in a workshop I can't begin to imagine.'

James came to the entrance and looked in, all the boxes he kept his bits and pieces in had been opened, and their contents thrown over the floor. The shelves had been pulled out and his table upended, the drawer had been removed and the contents strewn over the worktop. A little metal cupboard in the corner had been prised open and the contents left on the floor.

'Well, I'd better phone the police, not that they'll send anyone, they're much too busy persecuting motorists. They won't even be able to give me an insurance claim number as nothing seems to have been actually stolen. Come on, James, I don't want to leave your mother by herself.'

'Just a second, Dad, you go on upstairs and I'll lock everything up down here.' As his father went out the door James murmured to himself, 'I bet the sea gulls spied out where the spare key to the house was kept. Of course! That must be why the Duck Man was around, he was going to take the key when he saw me looking. I bet he came back after we went out.'

James went to the picture, took it down, opened the hatch and thrust his hands inside the gap. He felt the warm lumpiness of the blanket and lying on top of it the cold hardness of the lead encasing the key.

'They didn't find it, then,' said James, 'this time.'

Chapter Seven

THE three friends were sat in James' workshop. 'I'm so sorry,' said Geraldine, 'when you told me about the break-in this morning, I couldn't believe anything like that could happen in Shaldon. No wonder you didn't feel like going in for the rowing, you must have felt sick that anyone could do this to your family.'

'Are you going to clean up the room?' asked Mugsy, 'or are you waiting for the police to come and dust for fingerprints, or whatever it is they are supposed to do?'

'It is cleared up,' said James indignantly, 'you're as bad as my dad; he's always saying it looks like a bomb has hit it. This is all valuable stuff that's been put out ready to be worked on, it's not rubbish.'

'You didn't really say why you thought it was the Watchers that did all this, rather than ordinary burglars,' said Geraldine.

'Well, nothing at all was stolen, not even the money that had been left out on my Dad's desk, and whilst everything in the house had been turned over, my room had received the greatest attention. There's no sense to that unless the person was looking for something specific. If it were a proper burglar you would have expected everything to have gone, the TV, video, my Mum's jewels. Dad had even left his wallet at home as your father had said the meal last night was his treat, and I had a moneybox in my room with over £30 in it. It's a pretty strange thief that isn't interested in money.'

'Where were Digger and the key?' Asked Mugsy.

James went to the picture, took it down and undid the hatch. 'The house is built into the hill so it's got quite a large under-house, it's where all the pipes and electrics run.'

Mugsy stood up, walked over and peered into the darkness, 'yes, we've got one under our house as well.'
'My dad stores archive things to do with his office work in here, but it can only be accessed through this hatch,' James put in his hand, took out the bundle and placed it on the work bench, then put the key next to it. Then he unwrapped the blanket.

'So it's all still there then, but it looks like someone has vandalised poor old Digger though,' said Mugsy, 'he's all in pieces.'

'That was me,' said James, 'I was taking it apart by way of scientific analysis in order to discover how he worked.'

Geraldine cut in, 'James was saying he thought he could put it all back together and then fly it into the Ness.'

'Into the Ness? Won't it break?'

'I didn't mean into as in crash it into the cliff, I meant inside.'

'Wow! How are you going to do that?'

James replied, 'Well I don't think there's anything wrong with the mechanical. It will depend on whether we can use this key as a transmitter and control unit, assuming of course that it's got anything to do with the mechanicals in the first place. It might have a completely different use. But it does seem to be at the centre of everything,' he unwrapped the key as he spoke and placed it on a piece of paper. 'The trouble is if it is turned on, the controller in the Ness could presumably take control of it again, and as soon as we do turn it on it will alert the other gulls and Drum might come to avenge his mate.'

Geraldine looked at the splintered door and shuddered.

'I'm hoping I can figure it out, if it's anything like the controls on my plane it should be pretty simple,' said James.

'The one you crashed?' broke in Mugsy, 'and dissected and never put back together again?'

'Yes, that one, if I could change the frequency of the transmitter I could then control Digger by using that same frequency... the other controller would then be blocked of course.'

'Can you do that?' asked Geraldine.

'I've no idea, I was going to have a good look at the key when you two arrived.'

'How do you actually turn Digger on?' asked Geraldine.

James displayed the mechanical to Geraldine and pointed. 'By using this little indentation in the neck just here, I think, you press once to turn it on, and then again to activate it... it's a sort of multi-switch like the one on our computer that you have to press if it goes into sleep mode.'

Geraldine nodded. 'My uncle, the one who came with us last night, made his money in electronics, he's always buying gadgets - the more complex the better as far as he's concerned. Anyway, he's just bought a BMW and there's a sort of little toggle on it that controls hundreds of different functions - some of them marginally useful, so my uncle says.'

'Mmm,' said James, 'a sort of multi multi-switch,' he touched the indent gingerly, 'there's no toggle as such, but perhaps it turns. That should be on,' he touched it once 'and that should be activated. It's alright, nothing will happen, it all needs to be assembled before it will operate, so if I were to try and turn it this way...'

'So you say this would have been made by BMW,' said Mugsy, who hadn't been following the conversation very closely. 'Why would they want to build a seagull? It doesn't make sense.'

Geraldine sighed. 'No, Mugsy, dear, nobody's saying that, it's just an example of how switches can be multi-functional.'

'It's turning,' said James in excitement, 'if you turn it you can depress it again, presumably function and power, and turn again...He continued pressing. 'Right, I think I'm back to the beginning, how many turns was that?'

'Five,' said Mugsy.

'Six,' said Geraldine, 'you've also got the original setting.'

'I think the first setting is to power the thing up, I don't think it's a function button as such.'

'Put it back together again,' said Mugsy impatiently, 'I want to see it working.'

'So do I,' said Geraldine, 'but it would be nice to have some idea of each function before we start, one of them might be self destruct or something.'

'Gerry's right,' said James, 'I'll assemble everything first, then see if we can work it out. It's all been very intuitive so far, hasn't it?' He slid the various components back in place, frowning as he tried to remember the correct sequence, 'there are a lot more parts, I think, lower down in the body, but they're sealed off so I haven't been able to look at them.'

Geraldine picked up a piece of paper from the floor and a pen from the worktop.

'Right, deactivation function. I think that was press once to turn on and press twice to activate, didn't you say, James?' Geraldine wrote that down and looked up expectantly. 'What's next?'

'Then I pressed it and it all slid open, I was a bit nervous and did it at arms length,' said James, 'I don't think I pressed it from straight on in case it exploded or something. I pressed it from the side.'

'So function two is to deactivate and open.'

'No, I think it deactivates when it opens anyway, so presumably there is a second function to it.'

Geraldine wrote down as she said it, 'position two, open, second function…' She inscribed a series of question marks across the page.

'Hmm,' said James, 'it was a little awkward to work on, if I'd designed it I would have the bits that might need frequent servicing to be easily available, and the other bits, the ones you might have to work on less often, to at least be accessible but not in the prime position at the front.'

'So,' said Mugsy, 'open wide and open wider.'

'Yes,' said Geraldine, 'that could be it.'

'Yes' agreed James, 'that sounds logical, shall I try it?'

James put out his finger hesitantly, placed it in the indentation, gently pressed it, and immediately the bird opened out until it was virtually flat exposing all its internal workings.

'Wow! That's neat, how did it do that?'

'I don't know, I've never seen anything like it, now Digger's head hasn't gone flat has it, so presumably it's just the control console with no serviceable parts in it that need to be accessed. So if I turn and press this indent once, it should fold up to what it was like just now, and a second time should close it right up.'

'In theory,' said Geraldine.

'Yes, in theory, anyway, here goes,' James placed his finger in the indentation, and more confidently this time pressed it once, the bird closed on itself, he pressed it again and the bird reformed into Digger.

'That is such a neat action,' said Geraldine, 'it's like when the folding metal roof on a Mercedes is operated and it folds in on itself.'

'I've never seen one,' said Mugsy, 'you have probably get more of those in Surrey than we do in Devon. If you see a car like that down here you would know it's owned by a visitor.'

'What other functions would a control unit have?' James asked of no one in particular.

'Controls that actually move the bird and make it turn? asked Geraldine.

'No, that would be operated from the transmitter, you couldn't actually sit on the seagull pressing buttons whilst it was flying, could you? You'd want to do that from the hand held unit.'

'Send and receive?' asked Mugsy.

James considered this, 'I don't think so; a unit in a model plane would always be on receive. I can't see why it would need to transmit.'

'Change of wavelength for another operator to operate it from a different transmitter?' asked Geraldine.

'Yes, that could be it, the original transmitter could be lost or broken or they might need something more portable. It would make sense to have a spare.'

James put his finger in the indent, 'I'd say it is depressed slightly already, so if we're right, position one is for transmitter 1 –the one in the Ness - and position 2 for transmitter 2 – which might be our key.'

'Doesn't that leave a function?' said Geraldine.

'Yes, there's space for at least one more,' agreed James thoughtfully staring hard.

'Why don't we just press it anyway and see what happens?' asked Mugsy.

'No, suppose it's self destruct?' said James firmly.

'Well, why don't we just leave that function for now and try and fly Digger somewhere?' continued Mugsy impatiently.

'Yeah, well, there's a big problem, or two big problems rather. The first is that if this key is a transmitter we haven't got the faintest idea how it works, and secondly, even if we did know, we still can't see what the bird does, we'd literally be flying blind.'

'Yes, but think how cool it would be to fly a mechanical seagull,' said Mugsy enthusiastically.

'And suppose we crashed it on someone's car and they found out what it really was?' replied James patiently. Mugsy sighed.

'Why don't we try and work out the key functions and leave Digger alone for now,' said Geraldine reasonably, 'I've got lots of paper left.'

'What's the time?' asked Mugsy

'Just after 3.30.'

'Oh, plenty of time then,' said Mugsy in surprise, 'I was beginning to think it must be tea time, have you got anything to eat?'

'We need to leave at six o'clock for the treasure hunt by boat,' said James as he picked up the key, 'if it is supposed to be used with the mechanical it should have a similar sort of control function, but there's nothing obvious – the surface of the key all looks fairly smooth.'

'I think it fits into the palm of your hand,' said Geraldine, 'which leaves one leg sticking up like an antenna, at least that's what it looks like to me.'

'You said it was a barbecue handle,' objected James.

'That was before Einstein bravely captured Digger. I've re-evaluated it since then in the light of the evidence. What on earth are you doing, Mugsy?'

'We got a couple of doughnuts the other day, I think I only ate one of them and I put the other one in my pocket. Oh, it seems to be squashed.' He opened the bag and looked at the doughnut dubiously, 'still, it'll probably taste the same, squashed or not.' He took a bite. 'It's a bit hard,' he admitted reluctantly, 'as well as flat, and the jam seems to have seeped into my pocket, the material feels a bit sticky.'

'We're supposed to be scientifically analysing Digger, not indulging in a buffet,' said Geraldine in a disapproving voice, 'your hands are all sugary, look at them.' Mugsy absent-mindedly wiped them on his trousers and looked expectantly at James.

James nestled the key into his palm 'yes, it feels right I must say.'

'It's a different shape of course, but it's a bit like my

Playstation console,' said Mugsy, 'you sort of use your thumb and control everything.'

'I know,' said James a little bitterly, 'not that I'm allowed one, but it does feel right, the thumb is free to touch things on this right hand edge of the leg, should there be anything on the right hand leg to touch, that is.'

He brought the object right up close in front of his face. 'I can't really see anything obvious to press. Geraldine, what do you think? Do you want to have a try? Women tend to have more sensitive fingers than males, I've just got a slight impression in my mind that there are indentations down the side, but nothing more concrete than that.'

Geraldine took the key and nestled it into her palm and moved her thumb up and down. 'Yes there is something there, it's very faint though. I think there are four...no five indents, and at the top is something a bit bigger, a bit like that indent in Diggers neck - an off on switch perhaps. You obviously don't play the piano.'

'What has that got to do with anything?' asked James in bemusement.

'Well, men tend to use their hands like spades, with fingers and thumbs extended, you see it when they're bashing up a computer keyboard. If you used your bottom three fingers individually instead, you would feel that there are what seems like other indentations, as well as the thumb ones.'

'Press one,' urged Mugsy, 'go on, somebody needs to, press something.'

'Ok,' said Geraldine nervously, 'shall I?'

'Ok, press the top one, the one you think is off/on,' said James.

113

Geraldine moved her thumb, 'oh, oh it's...' She broke off.

'What? What's happening?'

'It just feels as if the key has come alive, it's gone warm...there's a slight hum as well, can you hear it?' she lifted it up.

'I think I can hear something,' said James. They all listened for a few moments as a distinct hum could be heard emanating from the key, its pitch steadily rising. James stood up, 'just wait a minute,' he called as he disappeared into his father's office and immediately re-emerged with something silver in his hand. 'Look, this is my dad's dictation machine, you can speak into it and it's supposed to be able to transfer your voice into typed words - if you plug it into a computer that's got the right software of course.'

'Voice recognition,' said Geraldine, 'my dad had it on his computer. He de-installed it when "Dear sir, I am in receipt of your letter" became translated into "feed the grey monkey with a piece of toast."'

'This one isn't much different,' admitted James, 'but the unit itself is designed in a way that is not unlike the key. What do they call it, intuitive and ergonomic or something? The dictation unit fits in the palm and the thumb operates controls you might need to use- volume control, forward, reverse - on the left side is a menu button. It's there because you don't use it as often, once you've selected something you'd generally just leave it like that whilst you do your work. Look at the little screen as I press this, as you can see it's scrolling through its various functions.'

'Hmm,' said Mugsy, 'but those are definite sorts of buttons aren't they? Not just indents that might do something vaguely useful on a good day. That's a long way from our key actually doing anything useful though. I still think if we took it to Mariners Weigh in the village they'd say, "Oh, that's something off a Johnson 10 hp outboard motor." Don't forget I am an expert on these things, I'm going to be a mechanic when I leave school.'

James looked up and nodded to Geraldine. 'Yes, give Mugsy a pile of old engines and scrap metal and he'll put together the most amazing contraptions. But this is far beyond old bits of scrap, Mugsy, it's pretty sophisticated stuff. Geraldine, why don't you try pressing one of the indents controlled by the bottom three fingers? It should select a function.'

Geraldine pressed gently with her little finger and immediately a shaft of light emerged from the top of the key.

'It's a torch!' exclaimed Mugsy, then continued in a disappointed tone, 'that's not very exciting, though, is it? We've got dozen of torches at home. Tell you what, let's go and get something to eat, it must be tea time by now.'

'That's not a torch light,' said James, 'shine it on the wall Gerry, hold on, I'll turn the room lights off, that's it, now put it at an angle... that's it.'

Mugsy muttered, 'What are we supposed to be looking at? It's just a white light. It's still a white light... Still a white light... Still...'

'Oh, Mugsy, put a sock in it will you, why don't you talk about something else whilst I have a fiddle with the key.'

'Like what?'

I don't know. Tell us about what character in history you would have liked to have been. Our teacher in primary school always tried that one when she wanted to keep us quiet for a few minutes.'

Mugsy became thoughtful. 'I don't pretend to know much about history you know, all I remember are meaningless dates, wars, the Normans killing the Romans, the Vikings killing the Egyptians, the 20th Century being all about everyone killing everyone else, but I liked the Romans, do you remember I was one in a play at primary school?'

'You were a Greek soldier,' said James scathingly, 'not a Roman.'

'Same difference, they both wore skirts.'

'So do Scots,' objected Geraldine, 'but that doesn't make them Greek or Roman, does it? Anyway, they're called tunics and kilts, not skirts. Whilst James is fiddling with that thing, why don't you tell us about your play - when you were a Greek soldier?'

'When I thought I was a Roman? Funny that, I'm sure it was a play about the Romans. I can't understand why it would be about them if I was actually Greek.'

James looked up 'Well, the Romans sort of took over from the Greeks, they displaced them, then hundreds of years later part of their empire used an old Greek city as its new capital. I remember now, it was a play about the fall of the Roman Empire, wasn't it?'

'The fall of the Roman Empire,' said Mugsy, 'what was all that about, then?'

They all looked on in astonishment as the light suddenly illuminated an area on the wall, around three-foot square. It flickered rapidly, then moved from light to dark and back again.

'Oh!' said James, 'I think we must have broken it, turn it off, quick Gerry.'

'That'll be this... yes that's it,' she said in relief as the light went out. She put the key down and scribbled on her piece of paper, then picked the key up again and looked round expectantly.

'What happened?' said Mugsy, 'it reminded me of being in a cinema when the projector breaks down - although no one has booed or thrown popcorn. If they did I could have ate some, I'm starving, it must surely be supper time by now.'

'Shall I press another indent?' Geraldine moved her little finger again and immediately there was a torrent of loud sound, like a rushing wind that rose and fell insistently.

'Turn it down!' shouted James, 'turn it down!'

Geraldine instinctively moved her thumb and the noise level reduced. She continued pressing and it dropped to a whisper.

'Volume control,' said James, 'so we know where that is.'

'So does everyone in Shaldon, I should think,' said Mugsy. 'Try one more indent,' he urged, 'it might then do something we can actually understand the purpose of... it might disgorge a bar of chocolate or something.'

'It's not a vending machine,' objected Geraldine, she moved her finger, 'there, has anything happened?'

'I don't think so,' said James uncertainly.

'I'll try another indent then.'

'Oh!' they all echoed in unison, as the dull metal of the key shimmered briefly, then displayed on its surface a screen about 2 inches square, with some sort of picture contained within it.

'What is it?' asked Mugsy, 'it's very mysterious, but I can't make out what it's supposed to be. I know! It looks exactly like that tin I gave you last Christmas, James, the one with hundreds of toffees in it, that I didn't get any of. Not one,' he finished bitterly.

'That's because you were away skiing,' objected James, 'you can't expect me to hold on to toffees for ever on the off chance you might want one at some point.'

'Holding on for ten days would have been nice though.'

'Stop it, you two, Mugsy is right. Mugsy, will you go over and pick up that toffee tin, it's over by the wall.'

'Why, surely you can't possibly believe James would leave any toffees in it after eight months, barely eight minutes would be stretching it.'

'Oh Mugsy, just do it will you. Do stop whinging.'

He stood up and walked over to the tin.

'Tell you what, don't pick it up, just touch it.'

'Touch it? I might as well I suppose, it's the closest I'll get to the toffees it once contained.'

'There, look! It's your hand, Mugsy... up on the screen.'

'Of course,' said James, 'when we thought that nothing had happened just now, you must have accidentally changed the transmitter over to this one here, and the second click activated the bird's eye - the camera. We're looking at what Digger can see from its perch on the worktop.'

'Just walk a few paces Mugsy and you'll be out of shot... there you've disappeared.'

'Just like those toffees.'

'Oh, don't keep on, I'll buy you a packet next time we're in the shop,' said James. 'Now we can see what the bird sees as it flies, we will need to learn how to get it up in the air and move it around. It would be almost impossible to control something like a model plane using just fingers and Digger is a lot more sophisticated than that. Is there an indentation or anything like that flat area you get on a laptop where you move your finger in order to move the mouse?'

Geraldine looked closely. 'Yes, there's quite a large indentation about the size of a 10p piece. It's much larger than the others. I thought it was just a part of the design, but everything else seems to have a use.'

'Try and move your thumb around in it... whoa! Not so mad!'

Digger had started flapping its wings madly and Mugsy just managed to catch it before it fell off the table and on to the floor. The bird stopped moving.

'Use the right hand side of the... yes, that's it, that's the right wing. Now the left, yes that's the left wing. Now if you keep your thumb in the middle that should be both of the wings together.'

'We can't do that in here,' objected Mugsy, 'we'll get knocked out by one of its wings, they're jolly big and strong. It's still only 3.45 you know, has my watch stopped? Surely it must be way past supper time by now.'

'For heaven's sake Mugsy, is food the only thing you can think about? Look at the wall clock, it's only just coming up to ten to four.'

'Well, I'm hungry,' said Mugsy defensively, 'it's not my fault if I've got a fast metabolism. Still, we've still got bags of time, haven't we, why don't we take it to that old look out tower that overlooks the grass by the Ness

House hotel? The one with all the picnic benches adjacent to the car park.'

'I don't know about that place at all,' said Geraldine. 'Where do you mean?'

'It's right at the top of the slope,' said James, 'and the trees have grown up around it now, I don't know if it was used by the coastguards or was a look out place during the last war. Teignmouth was targeted by bombers as it had a dock… it's only just round the corner from here. Hold on, I'll empty out the big blue rucksack that I keep the rowing things in and we can put Digger inside it. It's deep enough to ensure he doesn't peer out of the top, that'd be difficult to explain to passers-by.'

***

'Right,' said James, 'you seem to have a delicate touch, Gerry, do you want to be the pilot? Just try flapping the wings…that's it. Ha! That thumb movement makes his neck move… now his feet.'

'I'm just practising,' said Gerry, 'there's a noble tradition of pioneer female aviators you know, and I don't want to let them down by crashing a seagull onto a small child.'

'It's hovering now,' cried James, 'that's brilliant! See if you can move him round a bit.'

Gerry slowly brought the bird round in a tight circle and then sat it on top of the roof of the lookout. It moved its head at them inquisitively.

'Wow! You're a natural,' said Mugsy approvingly.

'Shall I fly it towards the Ness?'

'Is there any sign of the other seagulls?' asked James, staring all round expectantly.

'No, I can't see any, presumably the key doesn't alert the birds if it's being used as the primary transmitter.'

'Hmm,' said James doubtfully, 'perhaps if we're quick there shouldn't be any harm done I suppose.'

Digger took off somewhat jerkily, then as Gerry became accustomed to the controls she made it swoop and wheel and then sat it on top of the Ness House Hotel roof.

'Ok, bring him back here, oh, and turn on the camera,' said James. It will be great to get a bird's-eye view!' The bird took off and they could see through its camera eyes a view of waves, greenery and, as it turned, a car passing and several people picnicking on one of the benches just below them.

'I'll just fly it over the sea a bit more.'

'No Gerry, we don't want it to go too far out or...'

'Oh! I've lost control, what's happened?'

James retorted, 'Look, there are five seagulls surrounding Digger, they seem to be guiding him. Come on, try and bring it back or we'll lose him.'

'I can't,' said Gerry, 'I'm trying, but the controls have gone dead.'

The birds wheeled over the Ness. Through Digger's eyes they could see a large freighter moored offshore waiting to enter the port when the tide was full, a fishing boat chugging back into the harbour, two men in a red dinghy motoring gently out to sea, and then the sheer face of the Ness. There was then a quick view of trees as the birds climbed steeply.

'They're on the Ness itself now, close to where we had our picnic a few days ago. Now, they're sitting on the bench. Oh!' for a few seconds the screen went blank, and then they had a view of several seagulls that seemed to be walking down a passage. The birds moved to one side as the passage became broader to reveal a vast cavern. A large white object lay to one side, rounded at one end, with a small superstructure and an open hatch in the centre.

'The submarine!' breathed James.

Then the view changed as Digger altered direction, and for a few seconds was obscured by the other gulls again, then there was a tantalising glimpse of a figure.

'It looked like the boy,' said James uncertainly.

'And so does that one,' said Mugsy craning to view the screen, 'no, it's not, it's much larger, it's the size of that person we saw at the docks. The one that lifted that heavy piece of wood then disappeared inside the warehouse. That group he's in... there's four of them isn't there? They all look the same.'

A figure detached itself from the group and started walking towards the birds, Digger turned its head slightly and for a second they caught a view of something much larger than the white object. Silver, an elongated elegant shape with one fin rising along its centre line that had several figures clambering over it. Then the man bent over Digger and the screen went dark.

'He's been turned off,' said James.

Mugsy looked up, his face ashen, 'did you see what I thought I saw?'

James paused for a moment, licked his lips and said carefully 'you almost accused me of being a drizzoid when I thought I saw a submarine. If that was what I thought it was, people are going to think we're drizzoids to the power of 10.'

'What was it you thought you saw?' asked Gerry curiously, 'you two were in the way, what did you think you saw?'

'You tell her,' breathed Mugsy heavily.

'No, why don't you?'

'Someone please tell me.'

'I really don't want to... to say what I thought it was...'

'Nor do I,' cut in Mugsy, 'I'd rather pretend I didn't see it, unless James tells you first, and it was what I thought it was.'

'Tell you what,' said Geraldine impatiently, 'why don't you both write down on a piece of paper what it was, then you'll be independently corroborating each other if you've then written down the same thing.'

Mugsy looked at James and they both nodded.

Geraldine fiddled in her pocket and brought out the paper on which she had written the details of the various functions and controls of the key. She carefully tore a blank piece off the bottom, tore it in half then passed one piece to Mugsy, together with the pen.

He hesitated, and then using the wall of the lookout as a table, wrote down a few words.

Geraldine looked at James. 'Right, now you write down what you saw.'

James took the second bit of paper and followed Mugsy's example, 'the pen won't work, I'll just hold it up the right way for a second...OK, I've done it.'

Geraldine took the two pieces of paper and stared hard at the writing. Then said, 'I think we need to get back to your workshop James, if anyone hears me saying what you've both written they'll have me certified.'

***

When they returned to James's house his father saw them coming into the garden and came to the balcony to speak, as they entered the garage.

'I'm glad you're back, you'll never guess, but the police phoned up about the burglary, they're actually condescending to send a real policeman around about the matter, he should be here... Ah, look! Here they are, two of them...why do policemen always go round in pairs these days?'

'We've got to say something,' whispered Geraldine, 'this is all getting way beyond our league, I'm getting frightened.'

Dad continued, 'It must be because I met the new Chief Constable at that Chamber of Commerce lunch in Torquay last week, I always told you I was important, but no one ever listens.'

The policemen walked up the path and Dad came out the front door, had a few words on the step, then took them inside.

'We can't say anything now,' said James.

'We must,' said Geraldine firmly, 'I don't know what's going on, but I'm beginning to get a bit scared. I've never seen anything like that key before, nor anything remotely as sophisticated as Digger - its material and construction are outside my experience - and all those people that look alike, and the boy disappearing, and the Duck Man...Then to cap it all you both write down that you've seen a spacecraft. Look, this freaks me out, you must realise that some of these things we've got just don't belong on earth... and if there's a spacecraft involved as well.'

'Do you realise what you're saying?' Mugsy looked round him nervously, 'that there are aliens in the Ness? They'll lock us up and throw away the key, won't they? I would if I had a bunch of children telling me stuff like that.'

'Gerry's right,' said James, 'we've got to tell someone about all this, and the police seem the right place to start. There was another really strange thing though. You know that boy we glimpsed just now inside the Ness?'

'I know what you're going to say,' murmured Mugsy. 'It was Adam wasn't it?

'Yes, I'm absolutely certain it was. He wasn't drowned after all. Perhaps I did see the submarine as he disappeared. It must have rescued him.'

'Who's that?' asked Gerry, 'someone's just coming in your gate.'

'Oh, it's the paper boy, he's delivering the local evening paper, the Herald Express, Dad gets it in case he - or one of his letters - are in it, I don't think he ever is though. Thanks - I'll take that shall I? It'll save our dog shredding it.'

James unfolded the paper and glanced at the front page. 'Ha! Well in this case his delusions were real, there's a picture of dad – look!'

'Why should your Dad be on the front page?' asked Geraldine.

'No, not just him, there's dozens of people in it, it was at that lunch he just talked about, he's in the third row behind the new Chief Constable.'

'They could be penguins for all you can see of the audience,' said Geraldine.

'That penguin there,' said James pointing at one of the figures, 'that's Dad, at least I think it is.'

Gerry looked over his shoulder, 'I believe you, but there's a bigger photo of the Chief Constable at the bottom of the page… what's up James you've gone as white as a sheet? Now, are we going in to tell the police what we know?'

'There's no point,' said James, '…the new chief constable… Mugsy, come and look at his picture.'

Mugsy took the paper from James and stared hard. 'It's Adam, no, I mean the man we saw at the docks, or the one inside the Ness.'

James whispered, 'Clones, aliens, Watchers. I don't know what to call them, but whatever they are, the Chief Constable is one of them.'

***

'It's still hot, isn't it? You wouldn't think it was nearly 7 o'clock.'

'You're supposed to be reading the Treasure Hunt clues, not philosophising,' objected Mugsy.

Geraldine draped her hand over the side of Lucy Ann and let her fingers trail in the tepid water. 'I don't think remarking about the heat can remotely be seen as philosophising,' she observed.

'It's even hotter when you're wearing a life jacket and rowing like a maniac,' continued Mugsy.

'I offered to row.'

'It wasn't a proper offer,' said James as he pulled on the other oar, 'it was the sort of offer I make to my mum which I hope she won't take up…like asking if she wants me to do the washing up.'

'We haven't got a chance of winning though,' said Gerry.

'We might have if you concentrated more on the clues instead of talking about the weather, we can't read them and row, can we?' sighed James.

'Ah, you've hit the nail on the head there, haven't you? Why are we rowing when everyone else in the Treasure Hunt is using an outboard motor?' Gerry responded, raising her eyebrows.

'I just forgot to bring it,' admitted James, 'almost everything in the regatta is about rowing or sailing, so I just forgot that in this one you can use an engine.'

'Everyone else will be way up the estuary by now,' said Geraldine, 'we've barely got beyond Ringmore Towers, it's too hot and it's just about low tide and we're going to start scraping on the bottom of the river in a minute unless you keep to the channel more.'

'The channel winds about so much,' grunted Mugsy pulling hard at his oar, 'it's miles further going round all the bends instead of cutting straight across them. It's OK for you to complain about our straight route, but you're not rowing.'

'There's really no point in going on is there?' sighed Gerry. 'Why don't we pull into that little beach which the Templar way runs beside? It's fairy shingly and we can have a paddle there without worrying about sinking into the mud. I can't really concentrate on the clues and as I say there's not really any point, there's no way we can keep up with the other boats. They will be up to Newton Abbot by now.'

The two boys pulled towards the shore and as the bow grounded Geraldine leapt out and pulled it a little way up the foreshore. James and Mugsy got out and pulled it further up. They splashed about at the edge of the river for a few minutes then skimmed some stones which mostly ended up stranded on the sandbanks.

'What's that man doing over there, the one over by that bank under the trees?' asked James. 'He looks terribly familiar you know.' Then his voice dropped. 'Come away, you two,' he continued urgently, 'just pretend you're walkers out for a stroll on the Templar way and come over here, we can be round the corner in a second and get out of sight.'

They walked rapidly in silence for a minute.

'What was that all about?' asked Mugsy, stopping and staring at James as they rounded the corner and the figure disappeared from sight. 'Who was it, someone you owe money to?'

'If it wasn't the man from the docks who lifted that wood then disappeared, it was someone very like him.'

'Not another one of them,' said Gerry, 'they seem to be all over the place at the moment. What was he doing?'

'I couldn't really see that clearly, but he seemed to be putting something into the bank next to a tree.'

Geraldine peeped round the corner. 'He's still... No, he's walking away, he's got a boat pulled up by the tree. He's got in.' The sound of an outboard motor split the air.

'Quick, get behind this beached motor cruiser so he can't see us,' said James urgently.

The boat went past, steered by the man and following the course of the river; eventually it disappeared from sight under Shaldon Bridge.

'Come on, let's go and have a look at what he was doing.' James stood up and led the way.

They walked quickly along the shore towards the tree, 'the water's coming in quite fast now, we'd better pull Lucy Ann up a bit more or she'll float away.' Mugsy paddled over to where their boat was starting to rock gently as the tide came in; he pulled it up a few yards then returned. 'Which tree was it?'

'This one, I think, he was on this side of it.'

'The earth's been disturbed,' Mugsy remarked.

James bent down and gently scooped away the soil, 'it's not very far down, there seems to be something with a silver casing.'

'Don't move it, will you?' asked Geraldine nervously.

'I'll try and dig round it so we can see what it is. There…'

Mugsy whistled, 'it's a sort of silver ball.'

'There's a couple of spikes coming from it, they sort of look as if they're antenna don't they.'

'It's made from the same sort of metal as the key,' said James.

'What on earth is it for?' asked Geraldine.

'I don't know, we'd better cover it up again, I don't want to take it away or anything, it looks as if it has some serious purpose.'

'You know when we first saw that man at the docks, either this one or his twin brother?' said Geraldine, 'he'd been leaning over the side as if he was hiding something. I'd hazard a guess it was another one of these silver balls, where we are now is still fairly close to the docks, I wonder if the two are connected.'

'Come on,' said James, 'Lucy Ann is starting to float again, I think we ought to give up the treasure hunt, it's too hot and we're miles behind, let's get back and have a milkshake at the Beachcomber, it'll be open till late tonight.'

'Ok,' said Geraldine, 'I just hope the Duck Man isn't around, he seems to have it in for James.'

Chapter Eight

'That was a good morning's work,' said James with satisfaction, 'beating the adults like that in the Otter dinghy sailing. You were brilliant, Gerry.'

'Are you sure Mugsy didn't mind not helming? It seemed mean of me to pinch his place like that.'

'No, he was relieved to be honest, he much prefers rowing to sailing. Do you know the best thing?'

'What's that?'

'Alex didn't even finish in the first three. He'll be hopping mad, his dad didn't look too pleased either, seeing as Alex was helming for him.'

'I don't know why you two are always at each others throats, he's okay,' said Geraldine.

'You have him eating out of your hand, don't you?'

Geraldine blushed, 'it doesn't hurt to be civil to him; he's never done anything to me.'

James shrugged then pointed. 'Look, there's Mugsy! He's sitting in the garden at the Beachcomber eating something. Hi, Mugsy!'

'Hello, Gerry, James. You two were great. I bet Alex's dad wasn't pleased with him, he made a right mess of the race.'

'Not you as well, Mugsy, hey, aren't me and my dad competing against you two this afternoon?'

'Oh, no! What in?'

'There's a race for boats with an outboard up to 5 hp; you're in that as well, aren't you? Assuming you remember to bring your outboard of course. If you forget it this time you'll be disqualified.'

'Ha ha. I've already said I just didn't …'

'It's OK, I'm only joking.'

'I'm going to have a piece of chocolate fudge cake,' said Mugsy, 'to get my strength up, of course, not because I'm greedy. Are you having anything, Gerry?'

'No thanks; I said I'd pop back to our house and have some lunch with my Dad and plan tactics. Not that we need any if our competitors forget their outboards. What are we all going to do after the race?'

'I'd hoped we might go back to my house and have another go at operating the key,' cut in James.

'That's fine by me,' said Geraldine, 'what sort of time is our race going to finish?'

'Probably around 3.30,' said Mugsy, 'then I want to watch one of the last races, my Dad's in it.'

'What's he in, then?'

'Oh, just a race,' said Mugsy vaguely.

Geraldine unfurled a regatta programme, 'Which one?'

Mugsy looked over and stabbed a finger at the programme. Geraldine laughed, 'oh no wonder you want to keep it quiet - the "Old Characters trophy for regular patrons of local licensed houses!" '

'Well, we live near one,' explained Mugsy red faced, 'he pops in for 10 minutes now and again.'

Geraldine wiped her brow with her hand. 'Tell you what, if I go home after we've beaten you two into oblivion I'll have some tea, then come up to your house about six, that'll give us the whole evening.'

'Ok,' said James, that'll give us the chance to have a good long go at the key. I'm sure it's still hiding lots of secrets. You'll go past the shop, won't you? If I give you 50 pence would you pop in and get a packet of toffees or Mugsy will be moaning again all evening?'

'Ok, I'll see you at 2 for the race and don't forget your engine...'

***

'We're not at full throttle already are we?' shouted James above the roar of the engine.

'No, but we'll be disqualified if we break the harbour speed limit - that's only 10mph and we must be right on that now. We're quite light compared to most of the other competitors, so our engine is able to move us faster, we are in the lead you know...'

'Can you see Gerry?'

Mugsy looked behind him and the boat swerved as the tiller jerked. 'She's about 20 yards behind, she'll never catch us now.'

'And Alex and Bas?'

'If I keep turning round we'll lose our momentum. I think he was a couple of boats behind Gerry, he certainly won't catch us.'

'Watch out!' yelled James.

There was a loud bang and the Lucy Ann shuddered.

'What was that?'

'I don't know,' Mugsy cried, 'I saw something white, I thought it was a shark at first, it was going towards the docks.'

'It might have been a dolphin,' shouted James.

'No...When it was right under us I realised it looked metallic.'

'It's made a hole and we're taking in water, it must have been solid, perhaps it was an oil drum,' said James.

'The boat's filling up with water,' shouted Mugsy, 'Look there goes Gerry!'

Gerry waved wildly as she and her father swept past, followed a second later by Alex and Bas.

'We'd better try and beach her or she's going to sink,' shouted James.

'I think we'll just make it back to the river beach.'

'Gerry's won!'

'Good, now get bailing.'

By the time they arrived at the beach Gerry was at the waters edge, she grabbed Lucy Ann by the prow, 'it looks like you two just gave up when you realised that the awesome power of the Surrey Superstars was going to overwhelm you.'

'We hit something,' said Mugsy glumly.

'Oh, look! You're full of water... is there a hole?'

'Yes, towards the stern,' said James, 'that's the last race this regatta for the Lucy Ann I think.'

'What was it?'

Mugsy hesitated, 'James thinks it might be an oil drum, it was something pretty large, made of some white metal, it was well under the water and moving quite fast towards the docks.'

Geraldine looked at him strangely; 'But surely that would be going against the tide, oil drums don't have motors Mugsy.'

'But submarines do,' said James softly.

***

'That's odd.'

'What is?'

'I touched one of the functions we hadn't explored and the screens suddenly lit up.'

'Which one? There seems to be two screens, the one that's projected onto a surface, or the one on the key itself that went blank when Digger was turned off by the Watchers?'

'It's the screen on the key, Digger's screen... it can't be working properly, all it's doing is showing a smudged white shape.'

Geraldine came and sat next to James and peered at the screen, 'that's strange, why should it suddenly do that?'

'I wonder...let me touch that power button again, yes the screen's gone blank, I reckon it's a bit like a TV remote control, Digger was on stand by, not turned right off and I somehow turned him on. I'll turn it on again.'

Mugsy came and stood by them, 'move over, Gerry, I can't see anything, just white, are you sure it's Digger's screen and not something else?'

'Yes, I'm sure. The white... could it be that the gulls are all stored close together, and what we're looking at is a white seagull very close up against the camera?'

'Yes,' said James excitedly, 'Digger's looking straight at another seagull, right next to him. What a nuisance! Otherwise we could maybe see what was going on.'

'If we can see,' said Mugsy, 'you would think that we could hear it as well, if it's all supposed to be so hi tech. It's not like CCTV is it, where you can only see a grainy black and white picture? On those things no one can work out if someone's committed a robbery or is just eating a banana. This set up is very sophisticated; if you can see something in the middle of solid rock, you'd think you'd also be able to listen.'

'That's an interesting thought,' agreed James, 'Gerry, have we got that piece of paper on which we wrote down all the key functions that we could discover?'

'It's here,' Geraldine stood up and took it off the shelf above her where it had been wedged under a tin.

James settled the key into his palm. 'Logically sound is next to vision, so it should be the next indent round, that seems intuitive. We got sound yesterday, didn't we, in fact we were blasted by it, but that was on the large screen. Now, this is vision isn't it?'

'No,' said Geraldine, 'the next one is.'

'Sorry,' he moved his thumb 'so this could be sound.'

'Give it a try,' urged Mugsy.

'You always say that,' grinned James, 'you're just impetuous, right here goes… yes I can hear something.'

'It's very faint,' said Geraldine, 'use your finger to turn it up, that indentation there,' she placed his little finger in the right place.

'There, what about that?'

'It's still muffled,' said Mugsy judiciously, 'but it's a louder muffle.'

'Well,' said Geraldine, 'if poor old Digger is jammed into a corner surrounded by other gulls he would be muffled as well as blind. Can't we get the other seagulls to move a bit?'

'Hmm,' said James, 'If we got the other birds to come after us by using this key as the receiver, we might get Digger alone for a few minutes and we could see what he is seeing.'

'But surely Digger would just fly after all the others. He wouldn't stay behind would he?' said Geraldine

'Hmm, good point…this is getting complicated, if we turned him back to standby he wouldn't be able to leave with the others though, would he?'

Geraldine shook her head. 'The Watchers would notice, surely?'

'Not necessarily, I'm sure they're not staring at the mechanicals all day long on the off chance they might take off in order to spy on someone. If we did all this for, say, three minutes max, the other birds might have come and gone before anyone realises Digger is still sitting there. I'll give them a minute to leave, turn Digger on for the second minute, then turn him off again when we shield the key, so in that third minute the birds will return because they can't home in on us any longer. We might get to see or hear something whilst they're away, or perhaps the gulls might reassemble so they're not blocking Digger's view this time. Shall I do it now?'

'I've got no idea what you're going on about, but do it anyway,' said Mugsy.

'Hold on,' said Gerry, 'that's Einstein barking isn't it? We wouldn't be able to hear a thing with all that racket going on.'

'It's probably the paper boy, just wait a minute and she'll realise that her prey has escaped.' After a few minutes the sound of barking subsided.

'Ok,' said Mugsy, 'let's do it now.'

James grinned, 'that'll be the epitaph on your tombstone Mugsy. Will you time us? Tell us when each minute is up.'

'Ok I'll give you a countdown, just wait a sec as the second hand comes round, 5, 4, 3, 2, 1… go!'

James gave a commentary whilst Mugsy stared at his

watch. 'That's Digger in standby and the key in receive mode, the birds should be aware of us now.'

'They're not moving though. It's still a white smudge blotting out the screen. Perhaps it's broken.'

'Give them a chance, Gerry.'

'They're still not... Ah, they've moved! The white smudges are moving away.'

'Gerry, will you go to the window to see if they are coming here.' She got up and walked over to the window.

'30 seconds,' intoned Mugsy.

'Nothing... no sign of... ah, yes I think I can see them in the distance... yes it's definitely them.'

'I'll turn Digger back on for both sound and vision.'

'That's one minute.'

'I can't hear anything.'

'Shhh! I'm not surprised, if you keep talking all the time.'

'I'll turn it up.'

'What's that on the screen? Look, I can see one of the large Watchers, he's walking with another one, keep quiet will you, it's turned well up but they're whispering.'

They listened hard as a rather crackly voice said; 'Must this civilisation be destroyed like all the others?'

'It is the code, we must follow it, we have no choice in this matter, we do not have free will.'

'We must find the key before they discover our purpose, we are not ready yet...'

'There is a rumour about conflict with the rebels. Is it true?'

'We cannot talk of that here. Come to my room at the end of our duty.'

James said in dismay. 'He's walking away... not ready for what? Who are the rebels?'

'1 minute thirty seconds.'

'What can you see Gerry?'

'I can just see that person who...oh he's just gone out of shot. Wow wow!'

'Can you see the spacecraft?'

'Of course I can...it's fantastic! It's just like...'

'Two minutes.'

'Ok, I'm turning off.'

Gerry went back to the window, 'Drum's tapping on the fence post, no he's flown off now and the others are following.'

'I wonder why they all came?' asked Mugsy, 'normally they would all come only if they were needed as sort of reinforcements.'

'Perhaps the Watchers have become more desperate to get hold of the key.'

'That's three minutes.'

James stared at the screen, 'they should be back inside by now. I'm going to turn Digger on and off rapidly. Ah, they're back, we've got a clearer view this time, you can just see the nose of the ship. I can't hear anyone, though.'

'That could be because no one is around, if so, that's lucky for us.'

'I suppose... anyway, I'm turning off, I don't want to push our luck.'

'Well, do you believe us now, Gerry?' asked Mugsy. 'Was that a spacecraft or are we all having illusions?'

'Even though I've seen it with my own eyes I still don't believe it, it's just like the flying saucers you see in films. What did he actually say, Mugsy? I was concentrating more on the mechanicals than the Watchers.'

'Not much, but he seemed to be talking to someone else, not someone in control of the Ness, but certainly involved at a high level in some way. He seemed to have doubts, it was almost... almost conspiratorial, the way they were talking. He seemed to say there was a conflict with some rebels. I wonder if the rebels are good or bad... from our view point, of course.'

'So did Adam,' said James, 'he had doubts as well, so whatever it is they're up to, not everyone is in agreement.'

'Yes,' said Mugsy simply, 'but what is it they're planning? I've got no idea; it makes no more sense than when it all started. In fact it's got even more complicated. What's a space ship doing in the Ness, why are there clones, what's all this nonsense about destroying civilisations? Whose? Why? When? How?'

'Wow, that's a lot of questions,' said James, 'but I don't know the answers to any of them except the first. It's our civilisation, isn't it? They've destroyed other advanced ones, now it's our turn. Why, when, and how, remains a mystery though.'

'Perhaps that's where the key comes in,' said Geraldine slowly, 'Perhaps Adam meant the thing he hid was the key in the broadest sense of the word.'

'What?' said Mugsy, 'that's all a bit philosophical for a 13 year old.'

'Don't patronise me, Mugsy. Well, what I think I mean, is that perhaps Adam meant the key in the strict sense of letting someone in, but also that it is a key to the situation...you know, something vital.'

'Like I am the key to the success of my school's football team, but that doesn't mean you'd put me in a lock and turn me, does it?'

'Something like that Mugsy, the key is very important and perhaps it does a lot more than we've discovered or even dreamt about.'

'Like what?' demanded Mugsy, 'it already does a lot more than you'd expect from something that looks like a bit off a barbecue.'

Geraldine blushed but replied spiritedly, 'Or an odd piece off an ancient outboard engine. What I'm saying is that we only spent an hour or so investigating the various functions, and most of that time was wasted with your complaining about being hungry.'

'Oh, yes, thanks for the packet of toffees James. I'd give you one but I've ate them all.'

James smiled, 'and you had the cheek to complain about me scoffing mine quickly! Anyway, although we found several different functions that we understood, there were lots more indentations we didn't even explore, and do you remember that we went onto one function but didn't understand what it was all about.'

'Oh, yes that flashing light like a torch, and the noise,' said Mugsy, 'that was really weird.'

'That's the point I'm trying to make,' said Geraldine, 'there's a lot more to the key than meets the eye.'

'I remember,' said James thoughtfully, 'seeing a film once that had been speeded up. It was about an old-fashioned mail train going from London to Brighton in a minute or something. Don't ask me why. But anyway they speeded it up even more for a bit of fun, so it did the journey in 5 or 10 seconds and it was a bit like what we saw…just light and shade…darkness and flashing, and it was only when the film was slowed down again that the brain could realise what it was.'

'So are you saying we can watch movies on the key now? That's it's a portable DVD player or something?' Mugsy was scornful.

Gerry sighed. 'I'm just saying we know it's got a screen as we used it to watch the camera in Digger, and we know it's got sound capabilities as we could hear things. In that other function something was projected on to the wall and there was a continual noise that rose and fell. Perhaps that was sound and vision speeded up. There are controls to adjust those.'

James placed the key in his palm. 'It all seems completely intuitive… we've somehow known what they will do even before we press anything. What does our piece of paper say about the projector function?'

Geraldine retrieved the information from its place on the shelf and read it to herself.

'Well?' said James, 'what's it say?'

'I'm just trying to decipher it, the handwriting is terrible.'

'But it's yours,' said Mugsy aghast, 'are you saying you can't even read your own writing?'

'I was putting it all down very quickly, I just need to tune back in to my style, all great people have terrible writing, it's well known. Right, James, place your finger there - no, the indent below that one… no, below that. There are a lot of indents all around there, you need to have delicate pianist fingers like mine to recognise them. Yes, that's it.'

'Ok, so logically I should be able to control speed by moving my thumb down over one of these indentations.

It's this one we used wasn't it?'

Gerry looked at her paper, 'Yes, that's right, but we don't know what anything underneath the thumb function does.'

'Here goes,' said James. He pressed gently and immediately the light appeared on the wall again.

'Move it slightly,' said Mugsy, 'it's rather a thin beam, we managed to get it fairly broad before.'

'Like that? Yes, that looks right. It was this one for sound wasn't it?' He cautiously touched an indent and recoiled as noise assailed them all.

'Turn it down!' shouted Geraldine.

James said calmly, 'that'll be this one then, there that's better. Right I'll see if this will work to slow the flashing down a bit.' As he touched the indent an image formed.

'Wow! It is a picture, I don't know what it is though,' said Mugsy.

'It's not moving,' said Geraldine, 'I got the impression it was moving when it happened before because of all the flashes. Do you remember what we were doing? It's important that we get it back to those flashes.'

James wrinkled his brow in thought. 'Yes I do, Mugsy was displaying his only interest in history since asking our primary school teacher about England winning the world cup in 1966.'

Mugsy nodded, 'History all seems so pointless, let's just hope no one invents poetic history, that would be my worst nightmare.'

'I'll introduce you to Beowulf,' murmured Geraldine, 'that would scare you silly. Anyway, we've got this far, but now we're stuck. Think, James, what was Mugsy asking at the time?'

James leant forward. 'Yes, I remember, it was why the Roman Empire fell, and Mugsy seemed to be interested, not knowledgeable of course, but interested.'

Geraldine nodded agreement, 'anyway, that's when the light flashed, we might as well try it again as it seemed to work then.'

'Ok, here goes,' said James, 'why did the Roman Empire fall?'

The screen on the wall went blank, then a succession of flashes lit up the screen.

'Slow it down,' said Gerry, 'it's still way too fast, yes that's better, but it's still just a continuous noise.'

'Logically the sound should be... yes that's it. It's much slower now.'

'Is it the right speed though?' asked Mugsy, 'I don't understand a word, if they are words.'

'Mugsy's right, a picture would be universal, but surely the language could be changed if these people are... well if they're not from earth they presumably don't speak our language. They might need to translate theirs into various earth languages.'

'The tower of Babel,' said James.

'What's that?' asked Mugsy.

'It's a city where every language on earth was spoken, it's from the ancient world. Perhaps there's a Babel facility, hmmm, I can't see anything to press, there's nothing logical at all.'

Geraldine spoke, 'Do you remember the silly things the computer would type if you spoke into that software? The more you trained it by speaking to it, the better it was supposed to understand you. If there's nothing to press, intuition says you would instruct it to speak your language.'

'It could only do that of course if it's heard enough of it,' said James thoughtfully.

'Perhaps I should recite Hiawatha,' said Gerry, looking slyly at Mugsy, 'that must use every word in the English language and repeat it frequently... still, I couldn't really, I only know one bit, "Hiawatha's wooing", wasn't it called? I know that because we were going to be tested on it. But I never managed to learn the rest, it was just too dull for words.'

'There you are,' said Mugsy triumphantly, 'I said it was tedious - we had to learn it by heart at school.'

'I don't remember that,' said James, 'perhaps we might have read it through once in class, but I don't remember actually having to learn it.'

'Well I remember it,' said Mugsy with a shudder, 'every last word... it was part of a detention, do you remember? I was late five days in a row.'

'You only live two hundred yards away, Mugsy, how could you have been late every day?' sighed Gerry.

'I don't remember the reason, but I do know I had to learn it.'

'Still, never mind all that,' said James, 'we've done a lot of talking, if it does need to learn our language it should have heard enough by now. Perhaps we could ask it to talk in English. English language,' he continued confidently.

'Please,' said Geraldine.

'What?'

'If you ask for something you should say please.'

James sighed. 'It's a machine, anyway, nothing's happened has it?'

'You didn't really say it clearly though, it all sounded part of the general conversation and you do tend to mumble.'

'I don't mumble,' said James indignantly. 'I'm a very clear speaker.'

'Let me ask, then.'

'No, I'll do it, if you all kept quiet it might help it to realise it's a specific command. English language… please.'

The noise stopped.

'What happened to the Roman Empire?'

A voice came from the key. 'The Western Empire or the Eastern Empire?'

'Has it got a sense of humour or something?' asked Mugsy, 'what does it mean?'

James thought for a moment, 'It split in two, didn't it, after Rome was sacked, or was it before?' He spoke clearly to the key. 'Which empire was the most significant?'

'The Western empire.'

'Tell us about that.' He waited a second then said in a disappointed tone, 'it's not doing anything, is it?'

Gerry interrupted, 'I'm not surprised, you probably confused it, that wasn't really a proper question at all.'

'What are you saying?'

'That we need to be specific, as well as not mumble.'

'Ok, I'll try again,' said James. 'What did you have to do with the fall of the Western Roman Empire?'

'I am a machine. I am a tool in the hands of others.'

'That told us didn't it,' murmured Mugsy.

'Did the Watchers destroy them?'

'The Watchers are the tools of the Guardians and follow their code.'

'Stop!' Commanded James, then spoke softly to the others. 'We obviously need to be very specific, it seems rather pedantic. It appears that we've got to keep the question separate from the rest of the conversation, and make sure its specific.'

'And don't mumble,' said Geraldine firmly, 'not that you do, of course.'

James ignored the jibe, 'Right, here goes again.'

'What part did the Guardians play in the fall of the Western Roman empire?'

'That's sorted him out,' said Mugsy with satisfaction.

"AD324. Constantine reunited the empire under his sole rule after it had been split into an eastern and western empire for a short period. He created as the capital a city he named after himself, Constantinople."

'That's Istanbul now, isn't it?' whispered James.

"This city was founded on the ancient Greek city of Byzantium. Constantine was seen as a threat to the Guardians. Divided, the Romans power was greatly weakened and could be contained; united, they were powerful.

AD337. Constantine was poisoned by a Watcher; our advisers had believed this would cause the empire to be divided again between Constantine's three sons. We had expected this to be the end of the Roman empire for his sons were weak and quarreled amongst themselves. Do you want to see his death?"

'No,' said James, 'we'll do without that. Please can you show us the film and the sound, or whatever you call it, of what then happened?'

A brilliantly coloured film appeared immediately on the wall. It showed many horsemen running and riding across a large River, and the sound of shouting and horses neighing in terror. The machine continued;

"AD355. The Alemanni cross the Rhine and severely weaken Roman power in Gaul.

AD375. One of our Watchers led the Visigoths who attacked the Romans."

There was a tumult of cries and confused pictures of Roman soldiers fighting fierce-looking warriors; men stared out from the ground bearing fearful injuries and crying for help, whilst battle raged around them.

"The Watchers' army severely weakens the Romans and they are forced to accept him into their empire, enabling him to work from within to destroy them. There follows a period when the Watchers arm and train the enemies of the Romans and create a powerful force in the Vandals.

AD406. The machinery of the Guardians is used to freeze the Rhine."

'Stop! You have equipment capable of altering the weather?'

"I am a mach…."

'Stop. Do the Guardians have equipment that is capable of altering the weather?'

"Yes."

'Continue.'

"The Vandals and their allies cross the frozen Rhine, effectively marking the end of the Roman Empire in Gaul and making the empire vulnerable to further attack."

The pictures showed men in warm furs accompanied by pack horses walking over the bodies of Roman soldiers frozen in defeat, wearing little more than the uniform they used in warm Rome, caught out by the unexpectedly cold weather.

"AD407. The legions are removed from Britain."

'Look at those ships,' whispered James, 'there is everything in them; women, children, animals, they know they're leaving for good.'

A woman looked towards them and started crying, several children holding onto her clothes.

"AD 410. King Alaric of the Visigoths…"

'Look, it's a Watcher, he's identical to the ones we've seen.'

"….sack Rome, and during the following five years destroy Roman power in Gaul and Spain. Within 20 years, after pretending to work with the remains of the Roman Empire, the vandals conquer their North Africa territories.

AD 439. The Vandals capture Carthage…"

'Oh, it's horrible, they're just killing for the sake of it,' Geraldine looked away from the harrowing pictures.

'It's a slaughter,' said James softly, 'the Romans are trying to surrender but the enemy are just cutting them down.'

"Still, the Watchers could not be satisfied that the Roman Empire was irrevocably destroyed. They had shown a remarkable resilience over more than a millennium and had seen their empire reborn several times. Under the code of the Guardians the Watchers had to ensure the empire could not rise again. Their fears were realised when they sent a great army against Rome, led by a Watcher who had spent many years building up his forces…"

There was a tremendous noise and horses galloping and men shouting in pain and confusion. Several wagonloads of followers at the back of the Roman army screamed as a force of horsemen mowed them down.

"The Romans forged new alliances with their old enemies and destroyed the Watcher Attila..."

'That's Attila the Hun,' said Gerry in astonishment, 'he was bloodthirsty. Ohh, how horrible,' she looked away again. 'Tell me when it's over I can't bear it.'

"AD455. The Watchers had armed and trained another great force of Vandals, the Romans much weakened by their constant battles could do little more than look, as their forces were overwhelmed and Rome sacked and burnt..."

'There's the Coliseum, it's in flames... the city is being razed to the ground, there are great pits... the vandals are just spearing people and hurling them in, look some of them are still alive, they are trying to climb out, ohh!' shouted Mugsy.

"AD476. Romulus Augustus is forced to abdicate in fear of his life, against the threat to destroy every last Roman and their families. The Roman empire in the west was at an end."

The screen went blank.

'I think it's finished,' said James softly, 'I'll turn it off for the moment shall I?'

'Wow!' said Mugsy, 'Can any of that be true? They were really barbaric.'

Gerry stood up, 'it was so real, it was horrible...' she wiped away a tear.

'Are you OK?'

'I'll be fine, seeing everyone die like that... Watching a great civilisation just being destroyed so deliberately, so coldly. Why would anyone want to do that, what possible purpose could it serve for the Guardians, to make Earth fall into a state of barbarism for hundreds of years?' She wiped her eyes again, 'I'll be OK. Look, it's just after eight; I was going to have an early night anyway. I need a walk to clear my mind I've got a terrible headache. I need to think.'

'Do you want us to come with you?' asked Mugsy.

'No, why don't you continue to play with the Oracle?'

'The what?' asked Mugsy.

Gerry tried to smile, 'I thought you'd know about that, being practically an honorary Greek; it was the font of all knowledge at Delphi in ancient Greece. It knew the answers to everything. Anyway, I'll be off. I'll give you a call in the morning to see where and when we're going to meet up. Bye.'

Gerry went out and closed the door, James looked at Mugsy, 'she was a bit upset, wasn't she?'

'I'm not surprised it's… well, it brings history to life, doesn't it? Seeing it all happen and hearing those involved actually speak about the events. I hate them.'

'Yes, Gibbons took three volumes didn't he?'

'Who?'

'Never mind, he was just a bloke who wrote about what we've just seen, but he took millions of words to describe the decline of the Roman Empire.'

'It can't be real though, can it? I want to believe it's a Hollywood film. I was expecting to see Russell Crowe appear at any minute, playing one of the emperors.'

'I don't know if it's real, what we've just see is impossible of course, but then again the impossible seems to have become the norm in the last few days,' said James.

'I know you think I'm not interested in history and I'll deny ever asking this question, but what happened to the Eastern empire?'

'That limped on, but it was never as powerful as the combined empire was. We learnt about it last term, I did a project on it. The eastern empire gradually lost power until it was really only the city of Constantinople that was left, completely surrounded by the Ottoman Empire, although the crusaders liberated it several times. It was finally overrun in 1453 I think.'

'1453! But that's relatively recently. Wasn't that about the time of that bloke that discovered America? I remember learning a rhyme about the date he arrived. I had to do it for a detention. When did Rome start?'

'Around 700BC, I think, I'm not too strong on the origins.'

'So what's that? Over 2000 years that their empire lasted in one form or another? Wow! No wonder the Guardians thought they were a threat to them.'

'They achieved things that were never recreated again until relatively recent years,' said James, 'I remember being astonished when I had to research all their achievements.'

'Central heating,' said Mugsy, 'I remember that.'

'And concrete.'

'Concrete, are you crazy?'

'No, apparently no one surpassed the Romans' mastery of concrete until the New York skyscrapers in the 1920's. How are you for time?'

'I can stay for a bit, but I really don't think I can

watch any more battles…' Mugsy bit his lip and his voice quavered. He wiped a tear from his eyes, 'sorry, I'm being a bit feeble aren't I? Why? Why would they want to destroy those civilisations? Why do they want to destroy ours?'

He put his head in his hands and his shoulders shook as he cried softly, after a few seconds he sat up and wiped his face with the back of his sleeve.

'Are you OK?' asked James; he couldn't remember ever seeing his friend cry before.

Mugsy nodded and took a deep breath, 'I hate them, I hate them so much. It's real isn't it? This isn't a game… we've stumbled on something so big and I'm scared stiff. It just doesn't make sense either. When I was watching the fall of all those civilisations… well, they knew so much and then earth was thrown back into the dark ages. It took hundreds, no thousands of years, to crawl back up. If another race hates us so much why don't they just destroy us outright instead of… instead of playing games? It's like a cat toying with a mouse, it could kill it at any time but it doesn't. Have the Guardians got a grudge against us? Does it amuse them to destroy us bit by bit?'

James said, 'do you want to ask that? I don't think the Oracle would have understood what you've been saying, it wasn't really a question. I know just how you feel, it's a good job Gerry didn't see all that, she had her eyes closed, I'm not sure she would have coped very well.'

'I want to know some answers, but I'm not sure how to ask them. Why don't you try and find out some more things, but nothing to do with wars and destruction. I don't want to see any more bloodshed. I think I might write something down, try to get my thoughts in some sort of order. Where's that piece of paper that Gerry keeps?' Mugsy stood up and took the piece of paper and the pen from the shelf and sat back down again.

James sat still for a moment then spoke clearly, 'English. Who are the Watchers?'

"They watch the development of earth civilisations."

'Why?'

"To see when they need to be curtailed, if first they cannot be controlled and guided."

'How do you control and guide…? Give an example.'

"There are Watchers placed in many different levels of authority; when a civilisation approaches the threshold where the code dictates it must be destroyed, they seek to influence those who have placed their civilisation in danger. There are many examples of humans that they have needed to guide because they had inappropriate ideas. Archimedes, Leonardo Da Vinci, Brunel."

'Stop. We learned about Brunel at school, Mugsy, do you remember, it was in our last year at Shaldon Primary? He built a big house round here and built the railway?

Continue; in what way did you control Brunel?'

"Brunel was the greatest engineer that earth has produced, with access to modern materials, modern ideas and the energy to move the world forward at a rapid pace. At an early stage the code identified him as one who might need to be controlled and contained. He built great railways, bridges, and ships. It was believed he would hasten the creation of flying machines by three generations, and the time when the cordon would be broken was close. Brunel had ambitions to build The Great Eastern, a ship five times larger than any that had gone before, and the first vessel made from metal. The Watchers felt if that were successful it would give him the confidence to move on to even greater things.

His drawings were destroyed in 1853 when a Watcher employed at Russell's shipyard started a fire in the drawing office, which destroyed them all. It was thought this would break his spirit as he saw his dream disappear, but he strove even harder to build great things. The Watchers created a financial crisis and sent the bankers to re-posses the shipyard. But Brunel overcame these problems, enabling the ship to be built and launched in January 1858. Several Watchers were placed on its maiden voyage in September 1859. They sabotaged a safety valve on a water tank causing it to burst, killing five crewmen. This was a great blow to Brunel, who died within a fortnight. Our estimates of his technological prowess were proved right, as it was 50 years before another ship as large as the Great Eastern was built again. He would have hastened the ascent into space by half a century or more. The decision to curtail him was right, but others followed and the need to destroy your civilisation was merely postponed, not removed altogether."

The screen went blank.

'Space, it always comes back to space. Why? Are you OK, Mugsy?'

'I'm fine, I've written some questions of my own.'

'Do you want to ask them?'

'No, you carry on, I'm listening, it might help me to understand better.'

'English. Are all the Watchers in positions of great power?'

"No, we influence at all levels, but all roles have a purpose."

'Give us an example. A modern example.'

"Some Watchers are Journalists and others are commentators on the world."

'Stop. How can they affect a civilisation? Give us an example.'

"There are many now writing negative things about the exploration of space. They cite the great expense when the money could be used for more practical purposes like bringing clean water to Africa and feeding the hungry. They try to influence those in power and those who put them there. To put over the point that space exploration is not a desirable objective and that great things could be achieved if their ingenuity was channeled into other avenues. We have had some success in spreading this idea, but not enough. Mankind's' desire to explore space remains intact despite our efforts. He has an innate desire to reach for the planets then will try to reach towards the stars."

'Can stopping one great person prevent the civilisation being destroyed?'

"It is written in the code that the first option is to curtail humanity, not destroy it. Whilst we seek to achieve that by controlling original thinkers, the periodic destruction of great civilisations has proven necessary as mankind is always striving to attain what they can not be allowed to achieve."

'Has our civilisation reached that stage?'

"Yes. Its destruction is now urgent."

'Stop. I'm going to turn it off, Mugsy, my head's spinning.'

'That's fine by me,' Mugsy tried to sound cheerful but James could see he was very troubled. 'What can't we be allowed to achieve?' he asked softly.

'Are you sure you're OK?'

'I'll be fine; it's a lot to take in isn't it? One part of me is saying it's all absurd, but another part is saying it's the truth. I think I want to go home now.' He rose.
James nodded 'I'll give you a ring in the morning. I'll wrap the Oracle back up in its lead. I don't think I want to leave it down here, I'll put it under my pillow.'

Chapter Nine

'James, it's for you, it's Margaret.'

James sat up in bed and looked at his watch. It was gone 10.

'Margaret?'

'Yes, Gerry's mother, she's on the phone, she wanted to know what time Gerry would be home.'

'Home? How would I know?'

'Will you speak to her?'

'Ok,' he came down the stairs yawning.

'Hello? Yes… no… stayed here last night? No, it wasn't me… no, of course. I'm sure she will. Yes of course, will you let me know as soon as you hear something?' He put the phone down.

'What was all that about?'

'It's Gerry, she didn't go back home last night.'

'Not go home? But why did Margaret think she had stayed here?'

'She thought I phoned last night at about 10.30 to say you'd invited Gerry to stay here as it was getting too late to go home.'

'You didn't, though, you were fast asleep.'

'Of course I didn't. I hadn't realised I'd slept so late… I'm going to have a walk round to see if I can see any sign of her. I hope she's OK… Mum, I'm really worried. She was here until eight or so then went home. Why hasn't she arrived?' The enormity of the situation suddenly hit him. His knees buckled beneath him and he felt sick. He sat down and buried his head in his hands. 'We should have gone back to her house with her, but this is Shaldon, nothing could happen to her, surely. Besides, she had said she wanted to be by herself. She wasn't really in a mood for any company.' He wiped away a tear that was smudging his cheek.

Mum squeezed his shoulder, 'I'm sure she'll be OK, she probably just stayed with another friend and they simply forgot to phone her mum.'

James nodded and brushed his cheek with his hand. 'I'm sure it'll be something like that. People don't suddenly disappear, do they?' But why did her mum think I had phoned?'

'Do you want some breakfast?'

'I'd rather get off now and have a look around, I don't really feel much like eating.'

'You'd better get dressed first, though.'

'What? Oh, yes. I'll get arrested if I go off in my pyjamas, although during regatta week people do seem to get dressed up in all sorts of strange clothes, so I probably wouldn't be noticed.'

***

James walked down the hill and past the stone pillars that led into the Botanic gardens. He kept looking round, half expecting, half hoping, that Gerry would suddenly come running up and tell him... tell him what? That she had fallen asleep under a tree? That she had stayed with a friend and forgotten to phone? Gerry just wouldn't do that sort of thing, but if there wasn't a simple answer to her disappearance, what then?

He found himself at the river beach and walked slowly to his dinghy. There hadn't been a chance to repair the damage caused by whatever had hit them. The Duck Man was in the garden of the Beachcomber. He looked directly at him; James averted his eyes, walked to the dinghy and sat on the upturned keel, scanning the crowd that surged past him.

'I want to talk to you.'

James looked up. It was the Duck Man.

'I'm not a person to mess with; you have something of mine-now I have something of yours. If you return what is mine you will receive back what you are looking for.'

The Duck Man turned on his heels and walked down the beach.

James stared after him. What could he mean? He thought about going for a row to clear his mind and half turned the Lucy Ann over, forgetting it wasn't sea worthy.

'Oh, no, what' has happened to my fenders? I'm sure they were left under the boat.'

He let the craft fall back with a bang and stood up angrily. 'That's Alex's pathetic way of getting back at me, I bet.'

He blinked back some tears, rubbed his eyes with sandy fingers and took a final glance up the beach, hoping that Geraldine might suddenly appear.

'I can't just sit here,' he murmured, 'I've got to do something positive. I know, I'll go and see Mugsy, she might have stayed at his house last night after all. We do sound quite alike on the phone. Gerry's mum wouldn't know the difference, it's not as if we speak to her on the phone every day or anything.' He brightened, and walked off along the beach towards the Clipper, taking a wide berth at the outside tables where the Duck Man was selling some numbers to a visiting family. He looked up and gave James a penetrating stare.

He then walked along Riverside, glancing at the docks on the opposite bank, it didn't seem possible that only a few days ago they had been rowing over there, speculating on the disappearance of Adam, so much seemed to have happened since then.

James crossed the Torquay road at St Peter's church and walked along the towpath, past the new housing development before turning left towards the Shipwright's Arms, close to where Mugsy lived. He knocked on Mugsy's door, then rapped again impatiently, nervous of what he might be told. Mugsy's mother answered it.

'Hello, James, how lovely to see you. I hear you've got great hopes for some of the rowing races, Malcolm was so pleased you won the long distance race, of course you will need to borrow a dinghy now. Such a shame you ran into that metal barrel.'

'Is Mugsy... is Malcolm in? Oh, here he is - hi.'

'Hi!' His mother turned back into the house and James asked;

'Did Gerry stay with your family last night?'

'No, of course not, why, what made you think she did?'

James face fell and he sighed.

'What's up?'

'She didn't go home last night; nobody has seen her since she left us yesterday evening.'

Mugsy pulled the door to. 'Didn't go home, what on earth do you mean?'

'What I said, she didn't go home -she's been missing all night.'

'Ok, calm down, what made you think she was here?'

'Her mum phoned me this morning. She said I had phoned her yesterday evening at about 10.30 to say that Gerry was going to stay at my house. But she left us at around 8 o'clock, didn't she? I thought that her mum might have got you and me confused, we do sound similar on the phone. I had sort of hoped it might have been you.'

'Well it wasn't. Where can she have got to? Shall we go and search for her? I'm worried James, it's not the sort of thing she'd do is it, just disappear like that.'

'I've already had a bit of a look, but where do you start? She could be anywhere. I was going to go back home, she may be back at her house by now, most probably is. I should have brought my mobile and they could have phoned. Do you want to come back with me?'

'Yes of course. I'll go and tell my parents,' he returned a few minutes later, 'OK, shall we get off then?'

***

'Any news, Mum?'

'Hello, dear, you're back then; hello, Malcolm.'

'Hello, Mrs Smith.'

'No. I'm afraid not. Margaret phoned a few minutes ago-they've rung around all over the place but no one has seen Geraldine, what time did she leave here last night?

'About 8. No, a bit later.'

'That's long enough... Margaret's phoned the police.'

'The police? Surely that's not necessary, she'll be alright, won't she?'

Mum put her arm round James's shoulders and held him for a moment, 'I'm sure she will, dear. There must be some perfectly simple explanation. People just don't disappear like that, do they? Tell you what, whilst we're waiting for news why don't you go and do something to take your mind off things? I'm sure we'll get a phone call any time to say she's OK, so don't go onto the internet or you'll block any calls.'

'I don't really feel like going on the computer. Shall we go down to my workshop, Mugsy?'

Mugsy nodded and James led the way down, unlocked the door, went in and sat down in his swivel chair, then turned himself round a few times. Mugsy came and sat on the other chair. James stopped spinning and they both looked at each other.

'The police,' said Mugsy uneasily, 'I don't like the sound of that. Surely she's just staying with someone and forgot to phone or... or...'

'Mum's right, we need to do something to take our minds off it all.'

'It's a shame that Digger is grounded, we could have used him to look for Gerry.'

'You're a genius, Mugsy!'

Mugsy smiled faintly, 'I keep telling my teacher that, but she says my exam results tell an entirely different story. Why do you suddenly think that?'

'Just let me think a bit. You've given me an idea but I don't know yet how to implement it.'

'What? I don't know what you're planning. If I'm a genius I need to know why so I can repeat the experience.' They both smiled weakly, their gloom lifting.

'Well, last time we managed to get all the other five birds to come out of the Ness, but deliberately got Digger to stay behind. This time we just want Digger to come alone so we can use him like a spy plane. But I can't think how we could get him out of the Ness by himself.' He sat still on the chair for a few moments, brow furrowed in thought. 'If we can't get just Digger by himself, perhaps we could get them all to fly here. Then we could separate out Digger and somehow get him inside my workshop. Then we could turn off the transmitter. All the other mechanicals would then return to the Ness leaving Digger behind.'

'It's worth a try,' said Mugsy brightening, 'but we'll have to be very careful, I don't fancy being attacked by five mad mechanicals. Wait a minute, though. Surely we could do as we did before and turn Digger off so he gets left behind. Then when the others got here we could turn him back on and fly him off separately. It would mean we wouldn't have to try and separate him out from the others when they got here. I don't fancy being attacked with those beaks.'

James considered this for a moment. 'Perhaps that could be plan two. I'd be worried about leaving him behind by himself for a second time. We got away with it before, but if it happened for two days running one of the Watchers might get suspicious.'

Mugsy nodded 'Where's the key...the Oracle?'

'I've got it here,' James patted his pocket, 'I put it under my pillow last night but Mum changes the bed today and I didn't want her to ask any awkward questions.'

'And they'd be very awkward,' agreed Mugsy.

James pulled out the key, unwrapped it carefully from its lead covering and then put it in his palm.

'I'll turn Digger on and off quickly, we can see through the camera when it goes live if anyone is near who might get suspicious if he suddenly came to life. It's going to be tempting to leave it on, so look at your watch and give me ten seconds only.'

Mugsy nodded and stared at his watch.

James nodded, 'Ok, starting…now.'

'1,2..'

James said slowly, 'OK it's switched on, but the view seems obscured, something's in the way.'

'3,4…'

'I can just see the nose of the ship.'

'5,6…'

'There's someone sitting right by the…'

'7,8…'

'It's Gerry.'

'9,10…off'

James turned the Oracle off, hands shaking.

'What did you mean, it's Gerry?'

'She was sitting there, right next to the mechanicals. I don't think she was looking.'

'It can't be her, how would she get inside? We couldn't find any sort of entrance.'

James said slowly, 'the Duck Man…I saw him this morning, he said "you have something of mine, I have something of yours…" he must mean Gerry, he knows we're all friends and the something of his… surely it can only be the Oracle?'

They sat in silence for a few moments, James rocking gently backwards and forwards in the chair.

'We've got to go to the police,' said Mugsy quietly, 'this is just too big for us, it's getting really scary.'

'I know,' said James, 'but who would believe us?'

'We can show them the Oracle, that would convince them. There is nothing else on Earth like it.'

James nodded. 'Yes, you're right of course, but how did Gerry get inside the Ness? If we could find out we could try and rescue her. If we have to, of course we'll have to go to the police and let the Oracle go, but I'm not sure the adults will realise its importance. It might get put in a drawer for months and whatever is planned by the Guardians will have happened by the time they get round to examining it.'

Mugsy shook his head 'I'm not sure they'll fail to realise its importance, but whether it stays in the right hands is something else, we know they have people in positions of power, who knows who we can trust? If that Chief Constable is a Watcher he'll get hold of it, then he'll have the Oracle and Gerry and will know we're on to him. We'll just have to hope the Chief Constable doesn't get it. With a bit of luck he won't get involved in something like a disappearance.'

James nodded. 'Why don't we have another look round the Ness woods again before we think about handing the Oracle over? She didn't appear to be in any imminent danger, she was just sitting there.'

Mugsy nodded, 'OK, let's do that.'
'Hold on, perhaps we could just let Gerry know we have seen her, she must be scared stiff, so it would be a comfort to her if we could make contact.'

'Good idea, let's go for it.' Mugsy nodded assent.

'I'll turn on the camera first then try and flap one of Diggers wings gently to try and draw her attention,' he gripped the Oracle firmly. 'Right here goes, thirty seconds max, Mugsy, we don't want to endanger Gerry or let the Watchers know they're being watched.'

Mugsy undid his watch and put it face up on the desk and started counting off the seconds to himself.

James pressed the indent. 'Right, can you see her just over to the left? She's looking at something…probably someone is standing over by the space ship, here goes.'

'10 seconds. That was a jolly feeble wing flap.'

'I'll do it again.'

'15 seconds gone.'

James grasped his friends forearm and squeezed it urgently in excitement. 'Look! Gerry's noticed, she's staring at Digger – let's hope no one else is. I'll put on the sound in case she is able to give us a message.'

'20 seconds.'

Gerry looked round her then intoned…

Warning said the old Nokomis
Go not eastward go not westward
for a stranger whom we know not
like a fire upon the hearth stone
is a…'

25 seconds.'

'What's she doing now…? She's stood up…Someone's coming towards her I think.'

'30…turn off.'

'Well, we know where she is,' said James, 'but why would she give us a few lines from Hiawatha?'

'Perhaps she wants to wind me up.'

'I think she's got other things on her mind than winding you up, Mugsy, why didn't she tell us how to get in?'

'Perhaps someone was listening…It's a bit difficult to say turn left at the third rock if someone is standing next to you.'

The door to the workshop opened and James hastily put the Oracle out of sight on his lap and pulled the chair closer into the table so it couldn't be seen. Dad appeared at the door.

'The police have just phoned, it's about Geraldine, you're the last people who saw her so they want to speak to both of you. They'll be here in an hour.'

James nodded. 'We don't really want to sit around doing nothing, is it OK if we go for a walk, it might help to clear our minds and help us think of anything Gerry might have said or done?'

Dad hesitated;

'I'll take my mobile so you can contact us.'

'OK, that sounds a good idea, have you got any races on today?'

I don't think we really feel like… What's up, dad, you look rather pleased with yourself?'

'Do I? I didn't mean to. I'm as worried as anyone about Gerry, she's almost part of the family, she's the last person who would go off without telling anyone, but it's strange… I must have more influence than I thought. That man I met - the Chief Constable - he's coming personally to ask you questions, that's what I call taking charge. I'll see you later, then,' Dad went out and closed the door.

James had gone white-faced, 'The Chief Constable… He's a Watcher… we can't tell him. Not that we need to, he must know exactly what's going on, but why is he coming personally?'

'I should imagine he's hoping to get his hands on the Oracle as part of his enquiry, it's perfectly logical to ask for it. It would be impossible to refuse to hand it over.'

'Let's go. Shall we sit on that bench by the folly, I need to think.'

'OK.'

James turned off the Oracle and put it in its lead container. The pair walked down the hill to the gardens and turned towards the folly, where they sat on the bench. Several people were walking their dogs and he waited for them to pass out of earshot.

'It's still hot even at this time of the day; it's going to be a real scorcher later, let's move into the shade.' They moved to the bank near by and sat down on the grass where they could see the red cliffs of the Ness.

'I feel a bit helpless,' said Mugsy. 'We know where she is but we can't get in to help her. We can't really do anything else until we've spoken to the police, but I just feel we should be doing more than just sitting on the grass talking about the weather.'

James nodded. 'I know exactly what you mean. She gave us a clue but we don't know what to do with it. Why Hiawatha? She knew we were there, why quote Hiawatha of all poems?'

'There were other people there with her,' said Mugsy, 'we've already said she couldn't give us a proper message.'

'A message? Yes, perhaps that's just what she was doing, how does the poem go? I didn't really recognise the bit where she was quoting from.'

'That's because it was some way in from the start, it was from "Hiawatha's wooing", people often learn that bit, thinking they've learnt the whole poem, but it's just a small fraction of the whole... unfortunately. It's a rotten turgid poem. That bit is probably the most turgid of the lot.'

'You claimed that you knew it, didn't you? Well, it's time to prove that detentions work. Can you recite it from where Gerry started?'

Mugsy looked round him, 'I don't want anyone to know I can quote all of Hiawatha, it wouldn't be good for my image.'

'Oh, Mugsy, don't be so melodramatic. No one can hear you. Just quote it from where Gerry did, please.' Mugsy sighed deeply then intoned softly;

"Warning said the old Nokomis
Go not eastward go not westwards
For a stranger whom we know not
Like a fire upon the hearth stone."
Is a...."

That's where Gerry finished, no one heard me, did they? If they did I might have to flee the country,' Mugsy said anxiously.

James frowned. 'What on earth can it mean? Why would she quote just that bit?'

'She was cut off,' said Mugsy, 'she might have been going to quote more.'

But she quoted a specific bit, that must be the message. Why shouldn't we go eastwards or westwards? What has a fire or a hearthstone got to...Of course of course! We think the entrance is on the Ness. Do you remember Digger and Drum suddenly appeared out of nowhere when we had our picnic? We all said they must have been very close to have got there so quickly, it was as if they came out of nowhere. Now listen;

"Like a fire upon the hearth stone…"

'I think that Gerry is trying to tell us that the entrance is by that bench with the burnt mark from the barbecue. That must be where the birds appeared from.'

'Perhaps,' said Mugsy doubtfully. 'But perhaps not. Perhaps they were just lurking in a tree waiting to pounce on us.'

James hid a smile. Mugsy was always good at raising peoples spirits.

'Well, it all fits, we can at least go and take a look, we've got nearly an hour to kill before the police arrive.'

'We might as well,' Mugsy stood up.

The pair walked through the gardens, down to the beach, then up the path by the side of the Ness House Hotel, panting as the slope became steeper.

Mugsy groaned. 'Look, there's someone sitting at the picnic table.'

'It looks like visitors… Ah… they're going.' James waited whilst the family gathered up all their picnic items and walked past, talking noisily.

Then the two friends strolled to the bench and sat down, staring cautiously round them.

'Look, it said "neither east nor west" it can only mean we go north or south. It can't be north, can it, because the cliff edge is there? The entrance must be this way somewhere, very close to the table,' said James.

'There's not going to be a door or anything though is there?' Mugsy replied, 'we're not going to just stumble into it, surely we should try and use the key; that's what you use a key for, isn't it, unlocking an entrance?'

'Good idea,' James put the Oracle in his palm, stood up, then moved behind the bench, 'keep a look out Mugsy.' There was silence for a minute.

'What's happening?' asked Mugsy. 'I feel a bit of an idiot standing here like this.'

'I've pressed a couple of the indents that we'd already tried before-do you remember that nothing appeared to happen? I thought they might be something to do with that part of the Oracle that is a real key. Those indents still don't appear to activate anything though. I'll just walk behind this tree then round the bench to see if it's sending out anything like a signal. No… nothing… can you see anything happening that I've missed?'

Mugsy shook his head. 'Nothing at all. Perhaps Gerry just wanted to quote Hiawatha, knowing it would cause us to talk about it.'

'Perhaps, but Gerry is a logical sort of person, surely she would have had a reason. It's a bit bizarre quoting a poem in those circumstances unless you've go a good reason.'

'We'd better get back now or the police will be back at your house before we are.'

***

'The police phoned a few minutes ago, they're going to be here much later than they had originally expected. It'll be about 8 or so.'

'Oh, alright, thanks Mum.'

'…. and Alex phoned as well.'

'Alex? What did he want?'

'He seemed very upset that Gerry had gone missing, he asked if you wanted any help looking for her.'

'Oh!' For a second James was quite overcome, 'that's really nice of him, isn't it?'

'Why don't you give him a ring, it might help to mend some fences.'

'Perhaps.' James shrugged.

'I might as well go home for now,' said Mugsy, 'I assume we're not going to go in for any races or anything today. I certainly don't feel like it.'

'No, nor do I, it wouldn't seem right if Gerry's not there.'

'Do you want me to come back here later? It'll save the police coming round to my house if we meet them together.'

'I agree, there's no point in our seeing them separately is there? Why not come about 7 or so?'

'OK, see you later...'

Mugsy closed the door and Mum turned to James;

'You don't want to mope around all day; it'll just prey on your mind. Why don't you do something positive?'

'Like what?'

'I don't know, something to really occupy you, something that will take some time to do.'

James considered this, 'I don't feel like doing anything exciting. Just something really dull that I can get lost in. I know, I'll do my salt project for school and get it out of the way; if I don't it will be hanging over me all holiday. Then during the last week you'll want me to get my hair cut and get some shoes or something, and if the project is still outstanding it'll feel like the last week is a school one.'

Mum smiled. 'That's a good idea, you should be OK if you want to go on the internet to research stuff, I can't see anyone ringing us now, we know the police won't need to.'

'I'll leave my mobile on just in case though.' said James.

***

Mugsy turned up at 7.30. 'Sorry I'm late.'

'It's OK, Mugsy, I expected it, that's why I told you 7 when you didn't really need to come until 7.30. Shall we go downstairs until they arrive, then we can discuss what we're going to say to them.'

James peered into the living room; 'We'll just be downstairs until the police come.'

Dad nodded, 'we'll give you a shout... if Einstein doesn't alert you first.'

James led the way down. 'I don't think we should tell them everything,' he said, unlocking the door and turning the light on. 'Wow! It's still hot... it's like an oven in here. Look, I think we need to be cautious about what we say to them. If we let the police know about Digger and that we've seen Gerry and the spaceship, they'll realise we're on to them. It won't sound believable anyway to anyone who's not involved. We ought to be a bit cautious about what we give away. We could say that last night Gerry had told us she'd found a way into the Ness and had said something about going to explore it.'

'Probably through an old lime kiln tunnel,' said Mugsy.

'Yes, that's good, and we'll only hand over the Oracle if they specifically ask for it. I think we should play dumb, pretend that we don't know anything at all about it, other than we found it on the beach. If it appears that Gerry is in any sort of immediate danger though, we'll have to come clean of course.'

The door opened and Mum looked in, 'the police are here, do you want to come up?'

The Chief Constable was standing in the middle of the living room flanked by two other uniformed men. He sat down and let the others question the two boys, listening intently. James tried hard not to stare at him but there were so many striking similarities to Adam, as well as the man at the docks, the one planting something by that tree and the Watcher they had seen on the camera inside the Ness. The Chief Constable stood up and walked over to stand right next to James. 'You've made a couple of passing references to something you found on the beach, it might be important, can you hand it over so we can examine it? It might have some fingerprints or give us some useful clues.'

'It's here,' said James, standing up and patting his pockets, 'Oh, it seems to have gone. It's quite bulky, it must have fallen out when we sat down on the bench in the park.'

Mugsy stared at him, 'I think...'

'Don't you remember, Mugsy? I said I was worried about it falling out and I was going to ask you to put it in that zip up pocket you have.'

'I haven't got a......'

'When we were sitting by the folly, you must remember. Shall we go and have a look for it? It's only a few minutes away from here.'

175

'That's OK, sir,' said the Chief Constable, 'we don't want to cause you any more trouble. We'll go and look for it ourselves, where precisely do you think it might be?'

James groaned inwardly but said brightly; 'We were sitting on the bench by the folly, then sat on the bank by the side of it in order to get in the shade, then we walked back here. I must have lost it somewhere between here and the folly or on the bank.'

The Chief Constable rose. 'Thank you for your help, sir. If we can't find it we might come and ask you to help search. I'll come and find you personally.'

James shivered, 'of course, anything we can do to help Gerry. You just have to ask.'

The policemen followed the Chief Constable out of the door. Dad followed them and shut the door.

James and Mugsy looked at each other in dismay. James said with as calm a voice as he could muster; 'We'll just be downstairs, mum, in case they need us again.'

***

'Why did you say that you lost it? You put it on that shelf in the toffee tin when we came in a few minutes ago, it didn't fall out of your pocket at all. It's just there, look!'

'I wanted some more time Mugsy, Gerry wouldn't recite that poem for nothing, it must have some meaning to it. If we can't work the meaning out by the time the police come back we must hand the Oracle over to them and hope for the best. Go on, recite it again.'

'That's my worst nightmare, said Mugsy, 'to be condemned to an eternity of quoting Hiawatha. I'm only doing it for Gerry.'

'You said that Gerry might have been trying to continue with the poem but might have been interrupted. Can you just go on reciting the thing till I say stop, or fall asleep?'

Mugsy sighed, looked round as if afraid some school friends might be in hiding ready to pour scorn on him, then started hesitantly;

Warning said the old Nokomis
Go not eastward go not westwards
For a stranger whom we know not
Like a fire upon the hearth stone
Is a neighbour's homely daughter
Like the starlight or the moonlight
Is the handsomest of strangers."

'Stop there. What time did Gerry go for her walk?'

'Sometime after 8 o'clock, I think, why?'

'Almost exactly 24 hours ago. Don't you see, she would have got to the Ness just as it was getting dark; the poem says about starlight and moonlight, perhaps the entrance only operates at a certain time, at night. That would be logical; the Watchers wouldn't want every Tom, Dick and Harry to see them go about their business. They'd only come out through the cliff top entrance at night, say sunset to sunrise. She couldn't have used a key to get in of course. Perhaps the Watchers captured her or the entrance automatically opens if someone comes near enough. Let's go and try again.'

'What will you say to your Mum?'

'I'll say we've gone to see if the police have found the key…we would have helped them already of course if we had thought it would end up in the right hands, and if we don't find anything we'll have to hand it over anyway when we get back.'

Mugsy said, 'We'd better go up the hill and along the Torquay road, if we go the other way past the gardens we might actually bump into the police.'

'I'll take my mobile just in case,' said James.

They walked up the hill, down Ness drive then along the path beneath the trees that wound down to the Ness by the side of the golf course. James's mobile phone rang.

'Hello? Alex! How did you know my number? Oh, you phoned my home first… what? You want to help? That's really nice… yes I know you're very fond of Gerry, we all are.' James had stopped walking. 'Look, Alex, where are you now? By your dinghy? Look you might think we're mad, but walk straight along the beach and meet us outside the zoo. We'll see you in a few minutes.' He put the phone down whilst Mugsy looked at him in dismay.

'Why did you ask him? The fewer people know about this the better. Alex doesn't like you, how can you be sure he won't use the information to cause you problems?"

'He wanted to help. I know he can be a pain but he likes Gerry. Mum said about mending fences. We can't live in the same village and not bump into each other at some point. I'd rather we got on than continually sniped at each other. I will just have to trust him.'

Mugsy nodded slowly, 'I don't know why you two argue so much, you used to be fairly friendly.'

'I don't think the two of us are ever going to be best friends, but I've got a feeling we're going to need all the help we can get.'

Chapter Ten

JAMES was walking beside Alex. Mugsy could hear occasional snatches of conversation and, despite the circumstances, smiled when he heard the phrase 'mega drizzoid' used several times.

Mugsy felt in his pocket and touched the pieces of paper nestling inside. One of them was his own list of questions he had wanted to ask the Oracle. What was the other piece then? He drew it out and scanned it in puzzlement. It was getting dark in the deep shadow under the trees and for a second he couldn't make out what the paper could be. 'Oh, it's Geraldine's listing of the functions of the Oracle. At least I assume it is, I can barely read a word, she has got awful handwriting. She ought to become a doctor.' He stuffed it back in his pocket.

There were so many questions he had wanted to ask the Oracle, but yesterday he had been too sickened by what had been revealed to have the heart to ask them.

He murmured to himself as he trailed the others, James still talking at full pelt, Alex mostly just listening. 'Why? That's what I want to know. Why destroy our civilisations, allow it to recover only to knock it all down again? If they are our bitter enemies why don't they just destroy humanity instead of playing with it? It's like a cat playing with a mouse, but instead of killing it outright, this particular cat is just injuring it, then waiting for it to recover before playing with it again.'

'Did you say something, Mugsy?'

'No, just thinking.'

'You're a very noisy thinker.' James turned back to Alex then they carried on walking, the two of them talking intently. Mugsy resumed his thinking.

'Who are they? Where do they come from? What were the similarities between his and the preceding civilisations that meant they must all be destroyed? A high level of technological achievement? Why did the Oracle keep making all these references to space? What was it the Oracle had told them? That they were in danger of breaching the cordon. What cordon could that be?'

They crested the Ness and started to walk down the track on the far side towards the picnic bench. It was still warm. The sea could be heard as it sent a procession of waves against the rocks scattered at the foot of the Ness. Opposite, the lights of Teignmouth were starting to shine brightly as night gathered. A large ship lay out at anchor in Lyme Bay, ready for high tide so it could come into the Docks and load up with clay. The other two reached the bench first and sat down. It was almost dark under the trees.

'What do you make of all this, Mugsy?' asked Alex, 'I read lots of science fiction and I go to all the films, but this is real life. Things like this don't happen in the real world. You're a down-to-earth sort of person. It's all nonsense isn't it?'

'Why don't you show him what the Oracle can do?' said Mugsy, 'that's the best demonstration of whether this is all real or not.'

James hesitated.

'It's only fair, he needs to know what he's letting himself in for if he gets involved, he needs to know this is for real… that its not the latest Star Wars epic or anything like that.'

'OK, you're right of course. A few minutes with the Oracle will convince anyone. Can you keep a watch for anyone coming up from the hotel? I'll turn round a bit on the bench, then I can see anyone coming up from the other way.'

Mugsy moved a few paces so he had a good view of the path that wound up from the Ness House Hotel. 'What are you going to use as a screen, unless you intend to play it through the little one that's built in to the device?'

'That's really too small for two people to look at, Alex needs to be able to see the events properly.'

Mugsy looked vaguely around him, as if expecting to come across a screen that had been discarded in the undergrowth. 'You could use that tree trunk as a backdrop, it's pretty wide and smooth. It's getting pretty dark now, so he should be able to make out what is happening.'

James took the Oracle out of his pocket, unwrapped it, settled it into his palm and switched it on. 'Right, I'll angle it so we can… hold on I hadn't realised that, but if I put it at the right angle it projects into the air just around it. Look, it's 3D. We don't need a back drop at all.'

Alex was staring in amazement.

'What shall I show him?' asked James.

Mugsy considered this for a minute. 'The fall of the Roman Empire? No, wait a minute, you were going to ask it about Atlantis and other civilisations that had disappeared, but we couldn't face doing it, not after all we'd already seen. Why not try that now?'

James nodded, then realised Mugsy couldn't see the movement in the gathering darkness and spoke; 'yes, that's a good idea, keep watch but obviously you'll want to keep an eye on this as well.'

'Atlantis?' said Alex, 'but that wasn't a real place was it?'

'I don't know. We'll all see. English, what part did the Guardians play in the destruction of Atlantis and other ancient civilisations?'

"Byblos in Lebanon is the city that the code of the Guardians has caused to be destroyed the most frequently. It has had civilisations of some note for 7000 years. It was home in later years to the Phoenicians and Canaanites. They were artistic people who developed your alphabet. They built beautiful cities and had a great civilisation for millenniums. They were not a war-like people but the code showed their civilisations had developed to a stage where they must be destroyed, or they would threaten the power of the Guardians. They were conquered quite easily by assimilating them into the Persian Empire."

The Oracle had been displaying scenes of great cities that had wide avenues and statues that stood proudly in squares that were full of flowers and fountains. The scene changed as hundreds of Horsemen in leather tunics clattered into the streets, striking down all the people they could see. They rode into the temples in pursuit of those who tried to escape, screaming in terror as they fled. The horsemen wheeled round, toppling the statues and trampling the bodies lying on the ground.

"Their civilisation was completely destroyed by the greatest Watcher of them all, Alexander of Macedonia who you call the Great. He served the Guardians well and also destroyed the great cities of Mesopotamia during an extended campaign, thereby removing further threats. It is fitting his name should live on in many cities. When he was removed, it was felt wise to reduce the Greeks power by allowing the Romans to conquer them."

'Stop. You haven't said anything about the Egyptians,' said James, 'I remember spending hours at school learning about them. The Egyptians…did the Guardians destroy them?'

"No, they destroyed themselves through intrigue and famine before it was required to invoke the code. Their empire was weak when the Romans conquered them."

'Stop.'

'Jolly useful people, the Romans,' said Mugsy, 'they seemed to have a hand in everything. I'm not looking at the pictures any more, James; I'll keep a lookout and listen out for anyone coming up the path. We see all these great cities rise and then they are destroyed, together with their peoples… it's horrible.'

'Continue,' said James.

"Atlantis …"There was a pause.

'Go on.'

"That was the greatest Earth city of them all. 10,000 years before the Romans, they had a civilisation that was better beyond compare. They were the first great civilisation to rise from the seeds that the Guardians had originally planted and even the Watchers grieved when they followed the code and caused its destruction, although they are supposed to have no emotion. The people of Atlantis were no more than one generation from transgressing the cordon. The first to threaten to break out of their city and reach for the stars... so the Watchers had to urgently destroy them. Not with subtlety or through force of arms over many generations... but quickly and without mercy so they could never rise again. In modern times you now call them Minoans, but you asked of Atlantis so the story has been told using their ancient name. The Watchers followed the code and destroyed that civilisation utterly in the space of one night and a day. They caused their volcano, Thera, to erupt in a mighty explosion that could be heard all over the world. This unleashed a series of earthquakes and a tidal wave of unimaginable size and fury that overwhelmed the inhabitants and destroyed the land. Little is left to show the true extent of the achievements of those you term as being from Atlantis."

'Stop.' There was a silence.

Alex spoke slowly, 'My God, everything that appeared in the air around us was real wasn't it? Everything was taking place as it really happened. It wasn't a Hollywood type film with actors. It was more a documentary.' He walked round in a tight circle, staring round him as if the figures would suddenly return. His voice broke nervously as he continued talking. 'I could see the cities and the temples and the ships coming in to trade, and watch the volcano erupting and feel the earthquake as it rippled towards me. I had to hold on tight to the seat then, I thought I was going to be flung to the ground by the tremors. And the noise, the flames. I felt I was there when the tidal wave came. I saw the people fleeing in terror and heard their screams, but there was nothing they could do except run. They were overwhelmed by the water, the women, the children...everyone. They were just swept away as if they were pieces of straw on the tide. Who are the Guardians? Why would they do this? Who are they the guardians of... it's certainly not us, is it?'

'Those are some of the questions I want to know the answers to as well,' agreed Mugsy, who had turned back to watch the scenes as the tremors of the earthquake passed through their feet. 'Hold on, there's someone coming... a couple.'

A man and woman came toiling up the path. 'Good evening,' said James pleasantly, moving to one side to allow them room to pass the group.

The couple skirted the three boys nervously and continued up the path.

James waited a minute. 'I think they're gone. They've gone up to the viewpoint, I should imagine.'

'What was your plan?' asked Alex, 'you're supposed to be the clever one, if Gerry is really inside the Ness, how are we going to get her out? Shouldn't we go to the police or something?'

'The Watchers are all over the place in positions of influence,' said James, 'we don't know who to trust. We thought if we rescued Gerry, at least she'd be out of danger in case we managed to alert the correct authorities and... well, you can imagine what the authorities might do.'

'They'd go in all guns blazing,' said Mugsy, 'if they did believe us in the first place of course, that would be their reaction... to send in the army and air force and try and kill the Watchers.'

'Surely that would be a good thing though, once we've got Gerry out,' said Alex in a nervous voice. 'Surely we need to destroy them before they destroy us?'

'We'd be like a flea bite on an elephant,' said James, 'their technology must be far beyond ours. We can't fight them with our existing weapons. Anyway you can imagine the worldwide panic when it got out there were aliens and they couldn't be destroyed. This is an electronic age, the news would be around the world in seconds.'

'We'd do the Guardians' work for them,' agreed Mugsy, 'perhaps that's their plan, create mass panic and let us destroy ourselves.'

'But we've still got some time,' said James, 'they're not ready yet, the Guardians haven't arrived yet, or at least not most of them… we saw only a single spaceship, perhaps it was just a scout, I don't know.'

'Or perhaps it's stationed there all the time,' said Mugsy, 'there are occasional sightings all around the world; perhaps it's that one. It must go out and gather information so the Watchers know the stage of development the earth is at.'

'It's all very well talking and speculating like this, but what are we going to do about it?' asked Alex.

James replied, 'We think the entrance to the base within the Ness is right here, and that the Oracle can be used as a key to get inside.'

'And we think it has to be at night,' said Mugsy. 'Don't ask why, just accept it as the reality.'

'That's a lot of thinks isn't it?' said Alex. 'So what are you suggesting we do? Just keep on talking until Gerry is…'

'Gerry is what?' asked Mugsy sharply. 'What are you suggesting?'

'Well, they must have captured her for a reason mustn't they? They must know that others would come to look for her. Perhaps that is what they want.'

Mugsy broke in, 'Much as I hate to admit it, Alex is right, we need to do something. I don't like us just standing around talking, we don't know what might be happening to Gerry at this very moment. I vote we either try to rescue her now, or go to the police immediately - not the Chief Constable of course, we know he's a Watcher. Perhaps we can alert someone else in another police area or something.'

'It would all come back to the local police, though, wouldn't it,' said James. 'If the Chief Constable didn't realise before how much we knew, he would once he realised we had tried to bypass him and go to someone else.'

'So what are we going to do, then? Alex looked from one to the other.

James settled the Oracle into his palm. 'I'm going to try and switch the Oracle onto a different function, there's several we don't know the purpose of yet. We might be able to get inside the Ness, or perhaps it will turn out to be a weapon or something.' There was a pause.

'Are you doing anything, James, I can't see, I'm too far away?' said Mugsy.
'Stay there,' commanded James, 'you still need to keep a look out; it's a hot evening, there are bound to be people walking about. I am trying, but nothing seems to be... oh!'

A shaft of blue light had suddenly appeared from the ground adjacent to the bench, it was about 10 feet high, circular in shape and spun gently. Farther away, amongst the trees, a much smaller shaft could just be seen.

'Can you see that one over there, Mugsy? That must be how the mechanicals get in and out on to the cliff,' murmured James. His voice was very calm although his heart was racing madly.

Mugsy whistled. 'There must be some sort of mechanism that would ensure it doesn't open if anyone is near, but why put it right on a path?'

'It wouldn't have been on a path originally, would it? If the base inside the Ness was built thousands of years ago the sea would have been much further away and this place would have been well inland. It would have been virtually impenetrable with undergrowth. Alex, are you OK?'

'What the hell is that thing,' said Alex standing up and staring at the shaft. He took a couple of steps back. 'It might not have been you that activated it, someone might have done that from inside, perhaps they're coming out to capture us. I'm going home right now, I'm frightened, Gerry will just have to fend for herself. I don't want anything more to do with any of this.' He stood there undecided looking from one to the other, the last fragment of light shining on his eyes which blinked rapidly. 'Is anyone else coming? I don't fancy going by myself. It's getting dark.'

'It's a sort of lift shaft I think,' explained James nervously. 'Alex is right, someone might come out of it at any moment.' He stared transfixed at the rotating light for a minute. 'Mugsy, this is really scary. Perhaps we ought to go and tell the adults? Let them decide what to do.' There was silence for a few seconds then James took a deep breath and seemed to regain his composure for he said in a firmer voice. 'No, we need to rescue Gerry now before it gets taken out of our hands and they seal the place off or blast it to pieces.' He took a pace forward. 'It just feels as if you would just need to step into the shaft and it will descend into the Ness. It's intuitive, just like everything they do.'

'What are you going to do, James?' asked Mugsy nervously.

'Step into it, see, it's like a revolving door, but I think you can step in at any point.'

He walked forward, and was immediately encompassed by the blue light.

'Don't leave me behind!' yelled Alex and dashed after him, he was also immediately enveloped in the strange blue light that seemed to acquire a solidity as the figures entered it. Then the shaft started spinning faster and descended slowly into the ground, the two boys inside staring out, then beating on the shaft wall with their hands.

Mugsy looked on horrified, 'Wait for me!'

'We can't,' came James' faint voice. 'Take the key, keep it safe,' and the Oracle came hurtling out of the top of the shaft. Mugsy dived and caught it in one hand and lay there winded for a moment. When he turned back to look the shaft had vanished and only the grass and brambles of the ground could be seen.

Mugsy sat down breathing heavily, somewhere behind him an ambulance siren sounded, then faded into the still air.

'The Oracle…' He stared at it as if he had never seen the object before 'It needs to tell me what to do,' he brushed a tear away, 'how does the thing operate? I've never handled it.' He sat trying to regain his composure, staring at the spot where the other two had disappeared. 'I know! Geraldine's instructions…good old Gerry.' He brought out the piece of paper from his pocket, brushed away another tear then looked at the writing uncomprehendingly.

'I can't read it, her writing is so bad. I can't read it!' He grasped the Oracle and frantically moved his thumb up and down sobbing hard, tears falling on to the object. Suddenly the screen lit up, displaying a picture. Mugsy wiped away the moisture from the screen and peered hard at it.

'It's showing a large room, there's lots of controls, I've never seen anything like it…and that huge window, the sky is so dark beyond it…except… what's that? Is it a planet? It's blue and green. Oh! It's gone! We're turning…there's a red planet right in front…What's that noise?' He looked round then realised the sound had come from the Oracle. 'It sounds like rockets firing. We're coming in to land on that red planet….My God! I'm looking out from a spaceship. The Guardians…the Guardians - they're landing…it must be Mars. That other planet I could see… it was Earth of course. I've seen enough views of it taken from space.' The screen went blank and Mugsy stared at it for a minute as if willing the picture to return.

'English' he shouted at the Oracle, 'who the hell are you… what do you want… why do you want to destroy us?' Mugsy didn't expect an answer; he knew he had spoken too quickly to be understood. He stared again at the blank screen, put his head in his hands and murmured to himself, 'Dear God, who can I trust?'

The Oracle came to life.

"Trust in yourself and those closest to you, and remember that you are not without friends amongst the Watchers."

Mugsy flung the Oracle at a tree 'You're a liar! I hate you! I hate you all.' Then he threw himself on to the ground and began to cry.

Acknowledgements of Poetry used;

John Masefield; Sea fever
Alfred Noyes; The Highwayman
Henry Wadsworth Longfellow; Hiawatha's wooing
Anonymous; Do not stand at my grave and weep

The following books are available from Cadenza Press, please
visit cadenzapress.co.uk or email info@cadenzapress.co.uk

DANGEROUS FRIENDS

ISBN 1905363826

The all powerful Parallex Corporation has developed Glimmer
booths- enabling citizens to travel freely between Parallel worlds.
David is a natural Glimmerer who can travel without a booth.
Before his mysterious disappearance David's father owned Parallex.
His business partner Amos is the most renowned glimmerer of all.

The Parallels are collapsing into anarchy as glimmering allows
competitive worlds to attract commerce-ruining other economies by
encouraging vast transfers of power and money.

Mrs Baker seizes control of Middle World by enacting anti
terrorist laws to protect its citizens from a bogus threat. As Mrs
Baker draws ever greater powers to herself she summons forces
beyond all imagination to invade neighbouring Parallels. But to
succeed, Mrs Baker must first eliminate David.

He is framed for murder by a shadowy organisation opposed
to Mrs Baker and is blackmailed into helping them. He takes refuge
on Earth- still unaware of the existence of other parallels. But Amos
is in hot pursuit…

Dangerous Friends is the first thrilling novel in "The War
between Worlds" trilogy. The chilling resonances with modern day
Britain enable disturbing issues to be dealt with in a manner that
will appeal to older children and adults.

THE JIGSAW
AN EPPI SCOPALI NOVEL

ISBN 1905363834

Dwarves, goblins, wizards, homicidal megalomaniacs. The normal run of the mill residents that should make Eppi Scopali a pretty ordinary city of the outlands. Except for three things. The Great Staircase which enables inlanders and outlanders to traverse all the ages of the earth. Queen Zegga. And the fabled bridge of Dromond constructed from Elephants, some of them varnished – don't ask.

Thrown into the mayhem is Tom Ellis, who buys a jigsaw piece that becomes the most important thing in all the many ages of the world. Tom has another claim to fame. He lives just before the end of time. Much as everyone reading this book does.

Magic, humour, satire and the insanity of a Federation remarkably similar to our own dear European Union, make for an action packed story as Tom and his companions help (help!) in the struggle to prevent the end of time. Or at least make it as far as the Gathering, where the world's largest game of Zwaibichi - a fiendishly addictive card game - is soon to take place

The first part of a trilogy. Or a fourology. Who knows?

A SIMPLE ACT OF KINDNESS

ISBN 1905363540

The 6 day war. The release of Sergeant Pepper. New ideas, new values, new morals. It is the summer of 1967.

In the traditional mountain village of Leysin, the Schuber family come into a modest inheritance. Whilst they plan how to spend their windfall, their next door neighbour-beautiful, impoverished, and embittered Mrs Kandinsky-has her own ideas…

A wonderfully observed story of romance, deceit and revenge unfolds, as the truth surrounding the inheritance is revealed. The money becomes the catalyst for the destruction of long held beliefs as events spiral out of control, with tragic results.

WATER'S EDGE

ISBN 1846851637

When rat estate agent Sam, arrives at the house of field mice Mandy and Joseph, and brazenly tells them that their home is being sold for redevelopment by Reginald the Fox, it is just the start of the adventure…

Joseph has to find the 'freedom' document in order to prove their ownership. So why does he then give it to Sam, of all creatures? Why does Joseph then willingly allow himself to be imprisoned by the rats, together with Marvin the mole? Mandy makes the long and dangerous trip to Henley to enlist the help of the animal militia, but then appears to ally herself with the rats. To add to the confusion the animal militia befriend one of the rats, who tries to lead them into an ambush, which turns out to be just about the most confusing event of them all…

This is a charming and humorous adventure story, with lots of interesting animal characters that will delight younger children and their parents.

LIGHT AND DARK - SHORT STORIES

ISBN 1846851505

A collection of over 40 short stories split into two sections, written by Tony Brown. The 'Light' section contains light hearted tales that are amusing, quirky, surreal, light hearted. Dragons that fall through a hole in time, dogs singing opera, shadows that somehow get separated from their owner...

The 'Dark' section contains tales that are altogether darker, thoughtful and more poignant. The persecuted maker of Penny pipes, the man framed for murder by a hitch-hiker, the childhood sweetheart killed in an air raid. Choose the section that matches your mood.

THE RETURN OF THE DEVIL

ISBN 1905363818

Peter Williams- a failing English writer- is in Leysin, Switzerland, to research another novel, his last chance to save his career and marriage.

Miriam Hourbain is an archivist living in neighbouring Les Diablerets. 500 years previously her family were entrusted to watch for the return of a powerful Devil who had terrorised the Canton in the Middle ages. Local legend claims it was eventually entombed in the glacier of Les Diablerets by her forefathers.

Mark Stacey is a best selling American novelist residing in Les Diablerets to complete his latest blockbuster 'The Devil's Return.' Marks untimely death in a plane crash leaves Peter with the only remaining copy which he decides to claim as his own.

A series of frightening real life coincidences- including several chilling deaths-mirror the fictional events depicted in Mark's book. The novel forecasts the thawing of the devil from his icy tomb and the death of either Peter or Miriam as they try to prevent it...

A thrilling tale of the supernatural unfolds as the two principal characters struggle to avoid their inevitable fate.

Printed in the United Kingdom
by Lightning Source UK Ltd.
121351UK00001B/142-213/A